These stories emerge from a sensibility singular in its proportion of dreaminess to vigilance, merriment to mordant wit. And then there's the skilled sentence work, right down to the placement of commas. Frances Gapper seems to write from the very heart of the eerie everyday, and as you read this you'll be glad you joined her there.

Helen Oyeyemi, author of *What Is Not Yours Is Not Yours*

These are stories that are the lengths they need to be: they find their forms. The collection has a lovely patchwork effect. In reading this book you can sense a writer flexing all her muscles. She's unshowily showing us everything she can do, and giving us the real business of storytelling.

Paul Magrs, author of *The Ninnies*

I lay on my sofa, laughing, enchanted by its tone and the way it lifted me out of the cold English winter… There is no vagueness about this story. The writer tells us what she wants us to see, and we go with her, despite the bizarre nature of her journey. It's dreamy, but specific. It's a story inhabited by the dead and the naked, yet it's not silly.

Julia Darling, on 'Small Tall', *Mslexia*

I very much like Gapper's precise, startlingly odd short stories.

Ali Smith, selecting The Tiny Key as a book of the year in *The Guardian*

CW01498971

Also by Frances Gapper

Short fiction
The Tiny Key (Sylph Editions, 2009)
Absent Kisses (Diva Books, 2002)

Novel
Saints and Adventurers (The Women's Press, 1988)

Children's novel
Jane and the Kenilwood Occurrences (Faber and Faber, 1979)

Non-fiction
(as editor and co-author)
Gardens of England (A&C Black, 1991)

To walk *In the Wild Wood* is to enter worlds where the mundane is made magical. Loss of memory and self are rendered in dreamlike stories that owe as much to the lived experience of dementia as to fairy tale. In other tales, we learn of Sister Joy's obsession with spiders, or a funeral parlour worker who collects false teeth from the dead. Poignant, funny and astonishing, this collection showcases Frances Gapper as a story-teller working at the peak of her craft.

Frances Gapper is the author of six books, including three collections of short fiction. She has lived in various UK places, and had quite a few relationships, but at the age of 55 she married and sort of settled down.

In the Wild Wood

Frances Gapper

Cultured Llama Publishing

First published in 2017 by
Cultured Llama Publishing
www.culturedllama.co.uk

A CIP record for this book is available from The British Library

ISBN 978-0-9957381-6-4

Printed in Great Britain by Lightning Source UK Ltd

Cover design: Mark Holihan
Cover illustration: Jane Eccles (used by kind permission of
Graham McKinnon)

To Jane Eccles, my childhood friend and
dear Facebook companion
(September 1958 – February 2017)

and my mother, Patience
(September 1928 – February 2012)

and for Deryn

Contents

His Dead Wife

His dead wife hisses, this is your fault. You threw away the little white plastic wheel that fits in the strainer, because in your opinion it was fiddly and useless. And now look – as a direct result of your carelessness, nasty stuff has clogged the waste pipe, so nothing can go down. Horrible and disgusting. You slut.

I rummage underneath the sink. Don't you have a plunger, I ask her. She titter-screams, a plunger! A plunger would be no earthly use, believe me. You need to unscrew the U-bend.

Perhaps I'll wait until he gets home...

No! Do it yourself, right now!

Still on my knees, I discover a pack of twenty or so plastic wheels. From eBay, she tells me. Spares, just in case. Little did I ever imagine. What are you doing?

I lift the kettle. Making myself a cup of coffee.

You idiot, you'll just fill the sink up even more!

It's OK, I'm not spilling any.

Waiting for the kettle to boil, I turn my back on the sink. Not my job, or at least a distraction from my real work. I should be upstairs, writing.

I hear her pfft! – then a gurgle as the sink clears. Thank you, I say.

Pfft!

It's autumn. I carry fistfuls of dead leaves to the garden bin. Yellow, pink, orange and still-green. More keep coming down. I don't know what sort of tree it is, his dead wife won't tell me.

What I need, I think, is a garden vacuum. You fool, you'll wreak mayhem and devastation. The insects and worms, the plants, even a tree will be sucked up along with your leaves. And the topsoil! Can't you leave things alone. You are so obsessed with neat-and-tidiness.

You're the hyper-tidy one, I say, not me.

Indoors, yes. But I'm a child of Nature.

Ignoring my attempts to establish private space, she barges into my study and confronts me. What are you writing? Is it about me?

No.

Then it's shit.

She has very definite ideas about writing and her number one rule is, be honest. When will you be honest?

But she's not altogether truthful herself. One day she recites an old rhyme: first's the worst, second's the best, third's the dirty donkey.

In that case, I say, you're the worst and I'm the best.

No, because he was married to someone else before me. Aha! Didn't tell you that, did he? So I'm the best and you're the dirty donkey.

When I ask my husband about this, he looks at me quizzically and says no he's only been married twice. Once to her and once to me.

Early on in our courtship, he showed me a framed photograph of them together. And then clasping it in his arms he turned away, as though shielding her and their marriage from my intrusive curiosity.

He loved you very much, I tell her.

Yes, he adored me and I returned his devotion. She sounds unconvinced. But sadly I don't remember him at all.

It occurs to me I don't know my husband very well either. Sometimes I feel closer to his dead wife than to him. But, of course, she and I spend a lot of time together.

You snore, his dead wife informs me. That's odd, because I used to, but lately I've been wearing an anti-snoring ring on my little finger. Its silver bobble presses on an acupoint, result silence. And sleep for my husband.

Your snores keep me awake, she insists. The ones you deny yourself, the snores you should be snoring.

Well, I'm sorry, but obviously I can't please you both.

I know that. Do you think I'm stupid?

Moments later she resumes: people in my graveyard have complained, even the ashes of the cremated wish you wouldn't be so ladylike and discreet. Your non-snores are driving us all crazy. But *obviously* you couldn't care less.

November. Rooftop birds chirp, trill and click their beaks as though it's early spring. The slanting sun highlights my lines and wrinkles in the 1930s mirror, which belonged to his dead wife's dead mother. Another mirror, my own dead mum's, sits on the carpet, propped against the wall. That one I dust without looking in it, to avoid my past reflections. Mindful dusting. The result is crap, so I'm told.

Woman, you are old. His dead wife is about to carry on when I interrupt. Some bits of me are older than others, I tell her. The right and left sides of our faces age at different times, Leonardo da Vinci noticed that, or was it Michelangelo.

Pfft!

According to the five elements acupuncturist, I am metal. My face has colour, but it's overlaid by a white cold mist. Also I'm very quiet, a sure sign of a metal person.

I am metal too, his dead wife tells me. I'm very quiet.

Pfft, I'm tempted to reply.

Often when I'm thinking or remembering, she assumes I'm talking to her. Symbiosis, a merging of minds? No, she just walks in and out of me.

We frequently discuss death, I'm not sure why. The bliss of dissolution, his dead wife tells me, is like falling asleep times a million. If you could bottle that feeling, she adds, you'd make a lot of money. His dead wife is a businesswoman to the ends of her polished nails.

So don't worry, she says. Though in your case, death may come sooner than later.

What? Do you mean I'm ill?

But she just laughs.

Actually, I tell her, I'm more afraid of getting Alzheimer's than of dying.

Pfft! Remember what that nun, Mum's friend from drama school, said about Mum? She hasn't changed at all, the nun said.

What point exactly is his dead wife trying to make, I wonder. And why is she calling my mother Mum?

Your no-brain mother had kept the best part of herself. Because love remains when everything else has been destroyed. Look at me for an example. Hahaha.

What if I'm really dying? How terrible for my husband, to be widowed twice.

No problem, his dead wife says, he'll soon find another woman to replace you. But of course he'll never recover from losing me.

Let's go sailing in the bay, I mistakenly hear her propose.

4

In fact she's keen to sell stuff on eBay. Mainly her own precious things, not mine (Who will buy your rubbish stuff?) Her perfumes and tiny bottles. I find them everywhere – in my bedroom obviously, but also the cupboard under the stairs, garage, fridge. To me they all smell the same, of vinegar and decay. His dead wife tells me I have no nose.

However my skin lacks any intrusive smell of its own, so she lets me dab each fragrance on my wrist. After I've wafted it around, she gives her considered impressions. White flowers, orange blossom, tuberose ugh. An elegant Parisienne, walking two little dogs. The incense of prayer hanging in the apse of a cathedral. She stinks like a civet cat that has taken to streetwalking, as a wolf said nastily. Help me or I may slip away. Green marsh lily, drowned dankness. The eve of war. Buttercups and primroses, a fresh cowpat. Sincere words of love spoken by actors. The seedcases of horse chestnuts. Unicorn piss on snow. A candle floating downstream.

Online we specify size of bottle and whether edt, edp or parfum. We don't list the top notes, base notes, etc – they can look that stuff up for themselves, his dead wife says. A little sharp at first, we tell our customers, but lovely on the skin, once it's settled.

Mmm, this one I do like, she says. It smells of cunt.

Sortilège, to foretell the future by casting lots or choosing cards, a precious vintage fragrance by Le Galion. A recent eBay purchase (we prefer buying to selling). His dead wife watched in annoyance from an upper window as a man tried to deliver the package, then drove off again.

So now we're at the sorting office, collecting our Sortilège. Customers and post office vehicles edge in and out of the car park. We just miss a space – You fucker! his dead wife screams at the man who's beaten us to it. Then we nab another space by the ramp.

Hurry up and join the queue, she says. Or we'll be here all day.

I join a ragged feeder queue outside the glass-fronted public office; people are tightly coiled inside, waiting their turn at the hatch. His dead wife is still in my car, fiddling with the audio settings and the satnav. I wish she wouldn't do that. One day the satnav will divert me along a twisty unknown road, the sky overcast, a weird music playing, and when at last I reach home things will be all topsy turvy, me the ghost and her in charge. Not that she isn't already.

A young girl wearing a pink anorak with a fake fur collar dances in the leaf-strewn wind. Her mum in a plum coat, red dyed hair, watches the child fondly. I'm becoming irritated, only them ahead of me, and we could all squeeze inside where at least it's warm. Scenting conflict his dead wife suddenly joins us, she has a nose all right.

We'll stay out here where you can dance, the woman tells her daughter. Dancing's not allowed in there. The child nestles close, tipping her head back, eyes bright with love for her mum. Let's get married, she says.

His dead wife nudges me. Let's get married.

The moment we join the queue in the anteroom, she hops inside my head. Averse to a squash and to breathing other people's breath, instead she contemplates landscapes from the Japanese calendar that hangs by our front door, near the barometer whose needle points to stormy even when it's calm. Blossoming cherry trees, the moon caught in a pine, sand dunes, the sea, volcanic lakes. Nature.

Going home, the satnav takes us down a road choked with parents delivering their kids to school. I hope you never give birth, his dead wife says. Then a bit later, cheer up, instead of a baby you've got me

At last we squeeze through the bottleneck and whizz along the main road. That's better, his dead wife says. The world is terribly overcrowded.

We're still in the world, I remind her.

She replies obliquely, we are two empty pods in a space capsule.

At the supermarket, I pause to stare at a colourful display of sanitary products. Pink, purple, yellow and blue. They're all ultra, unless they're maxi or new superfoam. With or without wings. Should VAT be charged on them, when it's not on men's razors, is a current debate.

His dead wife says, I used to wear those.

I just stuffed myself up with toilet paper. Or when the flow was heavy, I used my mum's incontinence pads.

Ugh, she says, too much information. Away with that nasty mess. We are both ghosts now, unwomen.

A relief to be rid, of course. But still I miss it, the bloody badge of youth.

I'm reading a novel by Anthony Trollope. Lily Dale has been jilted by the love of her life and she spurns another prospective lover, choosing instead to remain single, an old maid. This is the wrong decision, but Trollope can't help loving her for making and sticking to it. Nor can I.

His dead wife listens as I read; by the time Lily says I must fall in love with you now, addressing her mother in an extraordinary scene, we're all in tears. I understand, his dead wife says. She is mistaken, but heroic.

I must fall in love with you now, I say.

Nonsense. Pull yourself together.

We lie in bed together, me and my husband. He has curly hair, once blond, now grey. His face is creased by sleep and age. He's become familiar, at least I think I know him well, but of course I don't, because who really knows anybody else? But I should at least be certain of his appearance. When we first started dating, I found it hard to fix his face in my mind. Recently his dead wife challenged me to describe him and laughed at my efforts.

He is flesh, touch, warmth. Not much talk, challenging or sparking off each other, for that I have her. They complement each other. Although I never expected a three-way marriage, this arrangement weirdly suits me. Like an unborn child – their child? – I float, I drift between death and life, sleep and awake.

Tying his dressing gown, he goes off to the bathroom. I continue to laze in bed. A starling perched on one of the fake chimney pots in this modern cul de sac makes a noise like car doors unlocking. Perhaps a migration call, because more starlings arrive and shuffle along the ridge. Meanwhile on an adjacent roof two pigeons are having sex. The starlings look at them in astonished disapproval.

He's not back yet, maybe he's gone downstairs. Filled the kettle and switched it on. Opened the fridge. Taken out the two-pint of blue top and my wholebean soya milk carton. Noticed or failed to, something wrong.

A lump of something, ice perhaps, knocking inside the carton. Clunk, clunk. Faulty product. Today I'll take it back to the supermarket, queue at customer service. Or maybe I should cut the carton open. Fish out the lump, examine it.

He's been gone ages. This morning he told me he loved me and that "You're first best, not second best." Memories of Her no longer intrude on Us, he reassured me.

I'm glad he said those nice things.

At last, tired of waiting, I push back the duvet and go in search of him. It turns out he hasn't gone far at all – here he is, collapsed on the landing. And his dead wife too, bent over him. Long black hair, dead white face, vividly materialised as never before. What are you doing? she scolds me. Hurry up and call the GP's surgery, tell them to send a doctor, we'll need a death certificate. And then ring the undertaker. Don't just stand there staring at me like an idiot, you fool of a woman. Pfft!

The Leaf that Wouldn't Fall

According to a branch message, one of our leaves is upset at the prospect of being let go. Tell it fallen leaves turn into compost, so it'll give nurture and life to future generations. If it likes to look at things that way. But no (sap reports back from twig to branch to central core), leaf still hanging on grimly. Sigh. There's always one. Tell it leaves must fall, separate, depart – that's why they're called leaves, ffs. Off it twirls, convinced by our spurious patter. And now we feel strangely sad. Bereft. It's like this every autumn, but we forget.

There Was an Old Woman

A song keeps going through my head, the one, you probably know it, about the old woman. *There was an old woman who swallowed a fly, I don't know why she swallowed a fly. Perhaps she'll die.*

Perhaps she'll die. The headmaster of my primary school used to sing this, accompanying himself on the guitar. He'd go round all the classrooms. The other song in his repertoire was 'There's a Hole in My Bucket'. *Then mend it, dear Henry, dear Henry, dear Henry...* But anyway, the old woman song. At first I can only remember a couple of verses, but then they all come back to me.

There was an old woman who swallowed a spider
That wriggled and jiggled and tickled insider her.

She swallowed the spider to catch the fly, (we all sang the chorus) *I don't know why she swallowed the fly. Perhaps she'll die.*

She swallowed a dog (what a hog!) to catch the cat, she swallowed a cat (fancy that!) to catch the bird, she swallowed a bird (how absurd!) to catch the spider, that wriggled and tickled... She kept on swallowing bigger and bigger creatures, until she died, no 'perhaps'. It was the horse (of course) that did for her.

The song keeps repeating itself in my mind. I wonder if the phrase *She'll swallow anything* could be rooted in history, i.e. were there once people – women – who really could and would swallow anything?

Swallow, I think. Swallow, swallow, little swallow. I swallow. I look up swallow in the *Shorter Oxford*, which I haven't yet packed. Gulf, abyss, corresp. to MLG *swelch* (also *swalh*) throat, whirlpool. A deep hole or opening in the earth. A swallower is a deep-sea fish with an immensely distensible stomach, which enables it to swallow fishes larger than itself. Appearances of the word in modern literature: He swallowed it in three gulps. They made him swallow the tablets. He kept swallowing as if he felt a lump in the throat. Thick forests seemed about to swallow them up. The beloved machine has swallowed your card. He swallowed all Anna's savings fixing up this house. Every moment swallowed up and forgotten. Franz's interest in socialism was swallowed up by his terrible anxiety. She'd done her best to swallow her anger and be nice to Ruth. I must swallow my pride and overcome my fear.

It's those bug-eating people, on that TV programme. That's it, I think. The poor grubs and larvae and pupae and beetles being eaten by minor celebrities. I'm an insect, get me out of here. I don't even have a TV, but it's in all the newspapers. Phil Tufnell, hailed as a new British hero – and as 'delightfully self-effacing' – for chomping five plates of ants, et cetera. After being sick, Tuffers went on to bite the body off a large maggot. His catchphrase: 'If you can't do it, you can't do it. If you can, happy days!' And he crunched a moth pupa that was just getting ready to unfurl into a beautiful moth. All very one-sided and no protests from the insect rights organisations which don't exist. Now if it had been kittens... Just as I'm thinking this, lying on a mattress in what will soon be my ex-bedroom, for I no longer have a bed or any other furniture, I'm starting again, shedding, discarding things like old bits of skin and hoping to be reborn, or simply for my life to change – just then, my own young cat jumps up to the window, kills a fly with a single blow of her paw and eats it.

She looks pleased with herself. It's the first thing I've ever seen her kill. Just like that. Happy days. Well done, I tell her. And I feel no compassion for the fly, no, none at all. The fly had to die. The fly is dead, eaten. The cat ate it. She has not (yet) been sick. And greater triumphs lie ahead – mice, birds, God help us.

There was an old woman who swallowed a fly, I don't know why she... I should ring my mother, to check up on her. She's been very ill. In fact, I think I'll ring her now. She's bound to be at home. She used always to be out, walking in parks or visiting friends, but now she's in. She has Meals on Wheels – these are stodgy, she says, with too much Bird's Custard. But she eats them. I think she does.

I ring her. Guess who's here, she says. Louise!

Oh, I say, is it a surprise visit?

Silence.

Just a moment, Mum says. In the background she asks, is this a surprise visit?

No, my sister says, I phoned you yesterday.

Mum comes back on. No, she phoned me yesterday.

The cat burps, or hiccups. My mother was in hospital last month, for blood transfusions and tests. She was sedated before the tests, but not anaesthetised. They put a camera down her throat – uncomfortable, she said – and one up her anal passage, for a colonoscopy. Then she had a barium meal, which I'd heard was horrific. Mum drank the barium like a cup of tea. They X-rayed her, tracking its progress through her body. But the end result of all these tests was, they found nothing.

How are you getting on with the meals on wheels? I ask.

I don't think they're really necessary, my mother says.

I had plenty to eat before. Lots of salad. And watercress sandwiches. But we'll see how it goes, she says – one of her little phrases, to pretend she's still independent and not under anyone's control.

Her fridge, when I last looked inside, was full of eye-drops and packets of watercress long past their sell-by dates. Been up to your old tricks again, the young doctor asked her at the West Middlesex. My mother looked alarmed. Sorry, he said, and giggled. It's Friday afternoon. I'll prescribe you some more iron tablets – here she interrupted, Now what about my eyedrops?

All right, sweetheart, the doctor said, irritated. But you'll get me into trouble. It's not really up to us. Which kind do you have? he asked. We brandished a bag of them, which Mum had insisted on bringing along. Three different sorts. And how many times a day do you put them in? She was uncertain. Once a day, she said. OK, he said.

The hospital pharmacists (women) called us back to the hatch and back again. They rewrote the prescription. Twice a day for these, they said, I'll write that down for you, and use these ones as necessary to relieve dryness. And we're giving you a month's supply of iron tablets, not fourteen days.

While we were waiting for the pharmacists to call us back to the hatch, so the prescription could be freshly puzzled over, other people kept coming along. They'd look up at the number in a box on the wall – it was 93, lit in red against black, like at a supermarket cheese counter – then they'd look at the hatch, then at the number again, then finally uneasily at me. Excuse me, they'd say, where do I get a number? I'd say, you have to ring that little bell, then someone will come to the hatch and take your prescription and then they'll give you a number. Thanks, the person would say.

All afternoon, Mum and I had been standing in the wrong queues, or waiting in the wrong seats, and now the moment I'd grasped one tiny little bit of the system, it was my job to explain it to everyone else. It reminded me of when I worked in an office in High Holborn and used to spend all my lunch break, and my popping-out times, directing tourists to the British Museum. Go along that road, I'd say, until you get to Museum Street. Oh, Museum Street, they'd cry in delight. Yes, I'd say, turn right along Museum Street and carry on to the end. Then you'll see the British Museum, the main entrance gates are just across the zebra crossing. I would picture the roast-chestnut sellers in my mind, but these I never mentioned. I kept to the point. My directions were clear and succinct. And the tourists were so grateful and I'd feel so much more useful than I ever did at work, I used to daydream about being retired and making myself a little placard with a map on it, so I could parade up and down High Holborn all day, directing people to the British Museum.

That's because he's not French at all, he's from Dagenham. I can hear our next-door neighbour saying this, forty years ago. In between directing people, memory keeps thrusting images and voices at me. A weak wall has broken and the past is rushing back, in mirror-pieces. Mum is there too, of course. Maybe it's the effect of us sitting so close. She's in a quiet dream. I'm thinking of the onion man, with his striped jersey and beret, pushing his black bicycle. The tightly plaited string of onions, hanging on our cupboard door. Very advanced for the 1960s, the French country kitchen look. Only it kept being spoilt by me, rubbing the brown crackly skins off the onions, to reveal their young shiny selves. Rustle, rustle – a thrill like biting my nails. Rustle, crackle. And my mum like a trapdoor spider, emerging from the back kitchen to slap my hands away.

The spider – I was collecting rose petals, a delicacy my rabbit seemed to appreciate, a change from grass and dandelion leaves. I was only allowed to pick up the fallen petals. Sometimes these were fresh, but more often brown-spotted and wrinkled like old skin. When I thought my mother wasn't overseeing me from the kitchen window, I'd pull loose petals, or fixed ones, from the heads of Peace and Fragrant Cloud. One day, one bad day, I pulled a whole rose. Then I looked down at my dress. There sat a huge spider...

I'm trying to get to sleep, but I keep waking up. There's a fly in the room. It's buzzing. *I don't know why. Perhaps she'll die.* I put my earplugs in, the ones I keep for defence against next door's TV and radio. He's ninety years old, next door. I seal my ears and now I can only hear the ringing inside my own head, like a burglar alarm when the owners have gone abroad and the other people in the street lie awake, disturbed and made helpless. An alarm that can never be turned off, that's always ringing behind and beyond all the world's other sounds. Although it's mine and personal to me, I don't think it'll stop when I die, no, it will go on forever, ringing and ringing in the silence of eternity. I remember the haunted holiday flat in Portugal, right by the cemetery, and Helen doing the washing-up, she was just thinking it's a pity there's no plug for this sink when a plug came flying through the air and hit her on the cheek. The fly is still annoying me. It keeps settling on me, on my face, my arm.

I get up. The moonlight is very strong, it's lighting up this room and the hallway. A floodlight, a searchlight. I open the bedroom door and the fly flies out. Then I open the kitchen door, feeling somehow the fly wants me to, and the door to the back garden. Out goes the fly. My mother is there, in the garden. She's lying in a sort of hammock, all made of spider silk, in a web between the trees. And there's the spider, a very large one, it's right on top of her, spinning her into a cocoon. And the most peculiar thing is, I can see all this very well, without my glasses. My mother looks intrigued by what's going on, not frightened. All around the garden, things are hatching. Pupae are pupating, throbbing. Even the moon is like an egg, distended, bulging at one end. New things, hungry new things, are being born.

Cleaner

It was an end-of-tenancy cleaning job. She'd been sent by the agency. On arrival, she looked around her in dismay, then set to work. The whole place was filthy, littered with discarded packaging and crawling with pests. Shuddering, she averted her eyes while following vermin control procedures. The agency had been remiss – this should have been done ages ago. However, at last all the bugs were dead. She vacuumed up the forests, siphoned the oceans, bagged what remained and put it all into deep storage.

It Was

Gemini, it says, your world is about to be turned upside down. You know it's already happening. By someone who. In the garden, stooping and pulling grass and weeds from between the cracks in the paving stones, you feel on the brink of old age, though freed from great anxiety, your tenants having gone.

You watch the tree shadows lilting on the wall. 2.30am and you remember the reason you came back here instead of sleeping at your mother's – to move the broken fridge and fridge-freezer 'to the border of your property', as instructed by the council. Barefoot under rushing clouds, metal grating on concrete, you move them.

So you're selling, they keep repeating to you, and when are you putting it on the market. One neighbour says you're a bloody fool. She means for giving up this suburban house to settle with your partner in the north. For choosing her, your partner. Oh Jane, you would have made some man a lovely wife, she says. You think, well it's too late for all that now. But what a time.

Don't think you wouldn't be capable; forget the illusions. Remember La Princesse de Clèves, it's just like that. The court gossip, the intrigues, the desire and the necessity. The abyss. If she lets herself. Don't believe a loyalty of years can't be destroyed by a word, a thought. Betrayal, the web on the stairs, the spider running inside your cupped hands, on your skin. You suddenly lose your nerve and throw it away from you; it lands somewhere in the garden.

Midnight blue

Mum and I were just setting off for the Alzheimer's Society Christmas jumble sale when I noticed the bird, perched on the gutter of a house opposite. Yellow with a white ring around its neck, a species I didn't recognise, but my brother Hughie probably would. On the point of going back inside to alert him, I decided not to. I count magpies, signs of good or evil fortune. To Hughie, birds mean so much more. They're all the world he's got now. He's vulnerable. And this bird – this rare and expectant-looking bird – had zeroed in on him, I felt. The hunter become the prey, the twitcher the knowledgeably identified.

Sinister – and so that's why I didn't call him. Plus, it had taken long enough already to get Mum out of the house. Booted, gloved, scarved and zipped into her padded winter coat. We crossed the road, threading between parked cars. "They've all got stuck," Mum remarked. "Now, where are we going? I suppose it doesn't really matter."

"To the jumble sale."

My beautiful sister-in-law. I'd always known/feared she would leave him; it was just, as they say, a question of when. No goodbye note or forwarding address. Hughie spent all night on the beach – they lived up in north-west Scotland, in an old fisherman's cottage – amid the crashing waves, in a force 8 gale, shouting "Maggie! Maggie!". Maybe if he'd called her full name, the version she preferred, she'd have been quicker to respond. Or maybe not. Maybe she was sick of life with Hughie, his bird obsession, all that hand washing – they didn't have a machine, for environmental reasons and because he was too mean to buy one – being taken for granted and maybe yes, she'd gone off with a guitar-touting, pony-tailed traveller she met in the pub. That was one local rumour. There were others.

Above the noise of traffic, chants drifting from the football stadium and planes coming in to land at Heathrow, I could hear snatches of a weird lament, a sea song, luring, enticing. I felt glad to be inland, well up-river from the Thames Barrier.

"How old are you, Mum?" my mother asked me.

"Nearly fifty."

"And how old am I?"

"About seventy-five."

"Well, you're much older than me. I'm just a little girl."

At the jumble, we bought pink and blue raffle tickets for a bottle of white wine, a box of toiletries, a soft toy – all faded and worn, gifts of yesteryear. The stallholder neglected to write our details on the ticket stubs, so I asked when the draw would take place. She thought around five.

"We can't be here then – my mum's got a flu jab."

"That's all right, dear."

"What if – " But she'd resumed her conversation with a fellow stallholder.

We proceeded to the bookstall, where I found Bob Dylan's *Chronicles I*, almost new, only a pound. I turned to where he says the truth is a cruel joke and so it's the last thing he's aiming to tell in his songs. What people hear depends on where they're standing. A former neighbour had buttonholed Mum and was talking to/at her.

The woman in charge of bric-a-brac said hello.

"Oh, it's you," I said, placing her after a few seconds. We'd met once before, in the paint aisle of B&Q Enfield, way over the other side of London. She'd not been wearing reindeer horns then, but paint-spattered jeans. Balanced precariously, she'd glanced down at me, looking up at her. "They don't know what they've got in here and what they haven't. It's disgraceful." Then a store assistant, mistaking her for a young boy, told her to get down from the shelves immediately.

"Did you find the right blue?" I asked. "Midnight Blue?"

"They had to mix it for me. Even then, it was still too citrussy. Can I interest you in some bric-a-brac? How about this wand?" She pointed to a cigarette holder.

"That's a cigarette holder."

"Or could be a wand. Now with a black dress, maybe 1950s, you'll be all fixed for tonight's supper party. I'm asking everyone. Open invite."

"My brother might like to come," I said. "He needs cheering up."

"I'm asking you, not your brother."

I felt bewildered by the changing nature of the supper party. "OK, so I'll pick you up at seven – " then the music coming over the sound system changed to an old folk song, about a seal girl, a silkie. Though the heating was on high in the community hall, my bones ached with a longing sadness. Perhaps I needed a flu jab, too.

The paint and bric-a-brac woman – I remembered now, her name was Mary, but she preferred Jo – shook the wand at one of the speakers. "Whose influence? I don't like bossy." The music changed back to Slade and she handed the wand to me. "Two quid; a bargain. It has to be a single coin – there, you've got one." She plucked it from my purse. "Yes, I'm going as an elf. I can see you as a wicked fairy."

"But I'm not wicked."

"But you have that potential." We both laughed, I wasn't sure why. She asked my address, I gave her Mum's.

The cigarette holder was rather fine – complete with fake reversible cigarette, one end whole and complete, the other about to drop its ash. I could get the dress from Oxfam. Maybe some wings?

Walking Mum back home again, I remembered Jo opening tin after tin with her car keys. "These are all warm blues. I need a cold blue." How enchanted I'd felt to be included in her search for the desired and desirable blue. How I could have stayed forever in B&Q, exploring and deploring.

"Well I think she's very nice," Mum said.

Hughie was slumped on the sofa, looking tired and unwashed. "I'm going to a party tonight," I said. "An elf is picking me up at seven."

"Enjoy yourself."

I turned the cigarette holder to fag ash setting and waved it at the TV. The Natural World disappeared with a pop and a faint odour of shorted electrics. I felt pleased with the success of my first act of wickedness.

"What the" – my brother, magically released from his lethargy, jumped up. But at that moment, a few pure notes drifted through the half-open window. (A window open in December? For the same reason we have air fresheners.)

"I hope she'll be kind," Mum said. We could only hope, and peer. Hughie was now outside, chatting animatedly to a dark-haired girl. She wore a yellow coat and white scarf.

A second fey, untrustworthy sister-in-law – not ideal, but that was Hughie's business, I supposed.

Lemon tree

Giving her a lemon tree, what does it mean? That you walk on a cold, foggy day along the high street to the garden centre, at a time when thousands of hoping-to-travel or in-transit people are stranded at Heathrow, exhausted, angered by poor communication, standing in queues, lying with their heads on bags. And Kate Middleton is spending Christmas not with the Royals but in Perthshire for (according to your sister's copy of the Mail on Sunday) 'several days of shooting and big family dinners'. And you're feeling sad, because of a missed love affair. It didn't come to anything. It never will, now. Everyone is being too grown up and responsible. And true, it would have been disastrous. You know that. But you still remember times, as when coming in through the front door, inattentive, your hand clasped hers, or up a stepladder in the kitchen, the way she looked at you and so afterwards you thought about it. She's given you something, or taken it away.

Spirit
You're telling me about the moment when the Baroness relinquishes her hold on Christopher Plummer and he goes out to say deep things to Maria on the terrace. The Mother Superior's song. And you think, you say, that's what life's all about. The long smouldering looks, the unrequited love. The text you sent me at midnight, the fireworks and my mum saying, I hope they stop shooting soon. Your aunt Rosa, the Franciscan nun. The voice you heard calling Mary! The dead woman who once lived here. Your name. And you asked me, did I call you.

My loves
My old love wrote to my new love and sent her a picture. My old love is still my love, the new one only longing and guessing. I saw the envelope with its second-class stamp lying on the kitchen table. I touched her name. The picture drawn by my old love, to thank my new love for her gift of art materials, was of a cat (our cat – stout, tortoiseshell) sitting between two bowls, waiting to be fed. It meant nothing, at least I don't think it did, but in my current predicament, the world is alive with symbol and meaning.

I remembered a film I'd seen long ago about a bandit queen in India, the scene of her being gang-raped, in a strangely civilised way, the men nodding to each other and holding up the tent flap. At some point during that scene, I walked out. I went to the ladies, then stood in the foyer. She, the real bandit queen, now a respectable businesswoman, hadn't wanted the film to be made. I felt angry on her behalf, then guilty for having come to see it. My love (a previous love) stayed and watched.

It was

It was magpies cackling madly in the street trees, some unlucky times only one magpie, but often two. It was morning and then evening, leaves and then none. But the grass still poking up between cracks in the paving stones. It was me putting out the recycling and the other rubbish and you taking the bins back in if I was away. Me seeing your red car parked out front. Me smashing the glass in the back door, the wind caught it, and us picking up the fragments and tiny slivers, and going to buy new glass from Hond & Langer in Winchmore Hill. It was playing charades, you acting out Exodus, first syllable sounds like, and me truly having no idea. It was Mum squeezing her fluffy bird, which makes a noise like a real chaffinch. It was Christmas and the time before, when Gina came to help you with the outside. And that night, sitting on the old patterned carpet by the radiator, we played Chinese chequers, draughts and The Merry Game of Floundering. You said I played the merry and kind game. You and Gina sleeping downstairs on your airbed and me off to King's Cross at 6am. Hearing you stir in the dark, Gina's murmur and you saying it's all right, go back to sleep. It was gas escaping from the tap by the fireplace and me ringing the emergency number. You hearing the ghost's 'Mary!', a woman's voice, you thought it was me calling you. And that back room was such hard, slow work, you told me, they don't want you to go. By then you were painting the bathroom door. I sat on the landing. Nowhere else to sit now except floors and I mentioned that, living apart, S. and I were getting on much better. You talking about *Guys and Dolls*, *My Fair Lady*, *The Sound of Music*. You driving me across London, to collect the portable heater from Mum's house. Mum gripping your hand – 'It's you!' The spider in your car, the one half-way up my stairs. Your texts, no kisses, one, two. You wallpapering the bathroom, us trying to reassemble the shower rail. Me not knowing what to do. You smoking on the back doorstep. You telling me, well done. Me giving you the hundreds of pounds I'd been keeping in the vacuum cleaner. Us both saying thank you. It was January, mild, the grass still growing.

Bluebeard's Daughter

After Dad forbade me to enter a certain room, I simply waited until he'd gone out. Then I unlocked the door and found my dismembered mother and sisters. Luckily I've always been good at jigsaws, so I began putting them in order. Anna wore a blue-stoned ring, I recalled, while Jane had a long second toe. Some bits were missing – I made do with objects fetched from nearby bedrooms; e.g. substituting a lampshade for Nora's lost head. Then having pricked my finger I scattered blood, restoring them to life. Assembled, they made a fearsome army. Together we awaited Dad's return.

In the Wild Wood

Mum bangs around the house like a giant moth. She's moving stuff from room to room. Junk mail, toiletries, postcards, photos, clothes and shoes, toothbrushes, combs and glasses.

I should get up.

This feeling that we're on a journey. We're going some place, Mum and I. Or do I mean somewhere. I think how strange, to live in a place called Where, although of course they spell it differently.

Asked by the doctor to say where we were, in what district, city and country, time and season, Mum had no idea. She kept saying, "This is my daughter. She's here with me. Isn't that nice?"

The doctor consulted her notes. "You're the eldest daughter?" I said yes.

"I suppose I'm the youngest daughter," Mum said after a pause.

I cut my mother's fingernails and toenails. I wash her fine white hair and cut it with the paper scissors.

"Your new haircut looks very smart, Mum."

"Well, we'll see about that."

"Lou is coming on Thursday."

"That's not for you to say."

In the garden, running wild: Rosemary for remembrance. Mint for eternal refreshment. Lavender for bees.

A magpie swings in the neighbour's eucalyptus. Then I feel anxious to see another magpie, but it doesn't appear. Two green parakeets fly past, screeching.

"I seem to have those nice things," Mum says, pointing through the glass at a tub of cyclamen planted for her by Lou. They've been in flower for months, since before Christmas. We're standing on the only part of her kitchen floor that isn't cracked, broken or missing – I think the tiles must have been laid on some unreliable substrate. The ceiling is damp-stained from where the central heating pipes leaked, before British Gas put in a sealant. The light bulbs keep pinging. Mum no longer worries, though, about house maintenance or finance. Dementia has mercifully banished Care.

She examines the photos on her mantelpiece – "Now who are all these nice people?"

Child in the park: "My mummy hasn't got a shadow."

"Look, it's on the grass," her mother says.

The psychedelic tattoo parlour Ouch! sells magic mushrooms and smoking paraphernalia. The African supermarket – packaged hair, yams, bonnet peppers, dried silver anchovies, prawns in red juice. The Albany fish-and-chip shop is closed. A 65 bus stop. Another 65 bus stop. On the corner of two main roads, a McDonald's advertising its new healthy McSalads. Mum says, "I don't think we'll go in there today." We wait for the little green man, then I take her arm. Half-way across the road, she stops. "I'm not quite..." She peers at our feet. Drivers stare through their windscreens.

We cross the rest of the way in synch – right feet, left feet. I'm just doing this to humour her. I hope they can see that.

The Arts Centre, a brick fortress incorporating an Indian restaurant. Sunday lunchtime, all-you-can-eat family buffet. A stray Alsatian sniffs the grass – Mum says, "Big dog". Five green parakeets speed over our heads in attack formation. Mum says, "Chirp chirp".

The tide's gone so far out, the river isn't water any more, hardly. It's mud, plus rusty, skeletal, decaying things. Mum says, "Oh it looks terrible." We've timed it wrong again. I should get hold of a tide table. But really I prefer the river's bony artistry, its naked, negative self. High tide, full-flowing, is wife-and-mother; low tide, spinster auntie. Monstrous, childless. Yet alive.

New developments, flats with balconies and river views. An octagonal church tower, boarded up; the swinging sign says Musical Museum. "That used to be an old church," Mum says. "Now I think it's given up being an old church." It's given up being anything. On the tower is a dark bush of maybe dead buddleia.

A young couple stop under a tree with a parakeet in it. While he's snapping it on his mobile phone, the woman excitedly points it out to me. She thinks it's a budgie. I say no, it's a parakeet. Very common round here. Flocks of them. "Really!" – she opens her eyes wide. I think but don't say, it's an infestation. Soon perhaps there won't be any other types of bird, not even magpies.

Now Mum's on antidepressants, she can walk a long way. Along the main road. Past the fuel forecourt – "I think I had a car," she says.

"Yes you did, Mum."

"I had a little car, which took me to America on an aeroplane. Lots of people kept jumping up and down, shouting 'Hi, Mum! It's me!' I thought, I'll just creep away very quietly."

She crashed her last car, a black Metro, while turning out of this very garage. That was before her cataract operations. Before her keys were confiscated and the car sold. Long before that, our family car was a Morris Thousand Traveller, light blue, wood trim. Its floor disintegrated. My mother failed her first driving test. My dad passed his. A shouter, a gesticulator, a pusher-out into traffic. But a safer (luckier?) driver than my hesitant and careful mother.

We edge around recycling bins and down a slip road to the old towpath – now a tunnel between the houseboats on permanent moorings and the camera-guarded walls of apartment blocks. Air-conditioning vents blow on us.

She's driving us up a mountain. Night is falling. The hotel was full, so we drove on, hoping to find somewhere else. We haven't looked at the map properly. We just wanted to go south, to the not-too-touristy places, the nice beaches. We forgot or never knew about the mountains of central Crete.

The road is narrow and sharp-curved. It's dark. I keep falling asleep. Whenever I wake up, there's the void, just inches from our wheels. Terror and guilt. My mother drives on carefully through the night, up and down mountains. This is her first foreign holiday. I'm the experienced backpacker. I told her it would be easy, no need to book a package.

Now just walking along the river path makes me anxious, in case Mum falls over the unguarded side. We go under the road bridge. Up steps, down steps, another transitional bit. This morning when I was trying to find her travel pass, she kept offering me a picture of some flowers. "Well I seem to have this, although it is quite out-of-date..."

Strand-on-the-Green. Office space for rent in a converted warehouse. Nancy Mitford's pink cottage, water patterns on her bedroom ceiling. Magnolia and wisteria. A row of elegant flood-prone houses with blocked-off front doors. For Sale signs and a notice announcing a limited number of vacancies at the Sailing Club. The path is very muddy – a Spring tide? Flashing spears of boats, maybe the Oxford and Cambridge teams.

The path ends. We've walked as far as possible, now we'll have to turn round and go back. But first we sit on a bench, in the warm light. Gulls wheel and squawk. I threw half a loaf of white sliced in the bin this morning.

I collected my mother from a police station in central London, after one of her disappearances. "Mum! Mum!" she yelled, flinging open her arms. "Where have you *been*?"

Mum sits very close to me on the sofa and the cat squeezes herself between us. Together we watch Lieutenant Columbo solve another murder. An old lady crime writer and rose grower is the killer. Columbo asks her for a rose for Mrs Columbo, she snips one. He says, "Excuse me, Ma'am" and "Did you just" and "See, I'm interested..."

Something on the news about bears in China; I'm in the kitchen. Mum appears, distraught. "What are they doing to those poor animals?"

I rush through and turn off the TV. "It's all right, Mum. The bears will be all right."

She sobs "I don't think they will."

"Don't let Venice fool you. Oh Frances, it's all a load of rubbish. Don't be taken in by it. Oh don't be bullied by these people" (now we're watching *University Challenge*).

CSI Miami. A baby is given back to its real mother, who immediately hands it to another carer, then speaks into her mobile phone – "I'll never use that nanny agency again." The kidnapper says she was trying to save the baby from emotional damage, the kind you can't see.

"Oh dear, I'm naked. I'm an old woman" – Mum after her bath.

❦

One moment you feel OK, the next moment you don't. "I've been having panic attacks," you say. Just saying panic attacks helps a bit. Other people get those too and they're not bad people, not people who've completely messed their own lives up. To eat anything you have to coax yourself, try a bit of this. You're drinking too much coffee. No alcohol, that's probably a good thing. And you should stop watching *Deal or No Deal*. It starts off so hopefully, with all the reds intact, but half an hour later it's all gone wrong, it's awful. Noel Edmonds urges the tearful woman to accept the banker's offer. You cry when the contestant loses, you cry when they win thousands of pounds. You're a bit near the edge, emotionally. You read a story about a woman whose new varifocals don't work properly. It's unbearable. You choose a dress for the Christmas party and take it to the fitting room. Shocked by your own reflection, you hurry away.

An old man is sitting in the waiting room. He must be at least 90, with rheumy eyes and jittery legs. You both wait ages, then Doctor Crowe calls him in first. The waiting room's practically empty now. Feeling truly terrible, you move to another chair. Doctor Crowe is very kind, you remember. Maybe you should tell her, not just about your eye problems. You've waited an hour now. You start worrying, what if she goes for her lunch break and you have to see a different doctor.

The same man repasses, but at first you don't recognise him. He's smiling, with colour in his cheeks, and walking jauntily. He looks forty years younger. If she can do that, you think, anything's possible. She calls your name.

❦

The minibus driver let down the folding steps. "Morning, Patience!" She helped Mum to board the day centre minibus and fastened her seatbelt. I waved at Mum, she waved, the other old ladies waved, the driver waved. Off they went. Back they came at 3.30. Peep peep peep – the bus reversing into our road, my heart lifting. Mum ate big cooked lunches, she joined in the games (Reminiscences, Proverbs) and the singalongs. It's a long long way to Tipperary. Two lovely black eyes. Oh kiss me goodnight, Sergeant Major. Sergeant Major be a mother to me...

Then it all went wrong. The day centre in dispute over Hounslow's cost-cutting measures. A new minibus driver, male, unfriendly. Mum returning in strange outfits; the driver silently handing me bags of wet skirts and knickers. Another old lady got off ahead of Mum and tried to fight her way into the house. Mum's link worker wrote in the report book, "Patience hit another client". A meeting was held: Mum banned from attending the centre. The GP prescribed Seroquel for Mum, antidepressants for me.

"What are you living on, Mum, today?" my mother asked me. I told her I wasn't sure. "I don't think any of us are sure, Mum," she replied sympathetically. "I think we've got a home upstairs. But Mum hasn't got a home at all." She added that Sarah, the agency carer, had died. "She fell over her feet. Poor Sarah. She was found lying in the corner of a bus."

After I've left the house – Mum lying upstairs like a statue on a tomb – I lock the front door, a habit, a precaution, though I don't think she's likely to wander again, but still. Two disappearances lasting many hours, two police searches, two eventual returns thanks to kind strangers have made me careful.

After I've driven away, for a while nothing much happens inside the house, except changes of light and shadow.

The cat's favourite patch of sun moves across the carpet, now without her, since she's dead, buried in the garden.

Robert, the bearded and heavily tattooed local agent for Wiltshire Farm Foods, lets himself into the house – he knows the combination for the Keysafe – and stocks up the freezer trays with Minted Lamb and Dumpling, Sausages in Onion Gravy, Country Chicken Pie. Mum pads downstairs in her blue fluffy socks and one slipper. 'Hello darling!' he greets her.

'Hello darling,' she replies.

'How are you?'

'Normal.'

Robert takes his cheque from an envelope on the shelf.

A vixen emerges from her burrow under next door's eucalyptus into the tangled wilderness of Mum's garden. Overgrown lavender, scraggy rosemary. She sniffs at the cat's grave; paws at the trellis weighted by heavy pots; retreats until nightfall.

The cat's ghost slips easily past all barricades and through the kitchen door; she drinks from her water dish.

I've unplugged the chemical air fresheners installed by Lou. Without them, the house smells meaty, and of cat sick and urine.

Mum's on the sofa, blanket over her knees. I ask her if she'd like to go to the toilet? Indicating her lower half, she says oh it's been really awful. Upstairs I begin unpeeling her. Shit. Her pants are full, her tights soaked brown. It spatters on to her lilac slippers. Is all over her legs. And on me now. I run a bath and pull Mum's light blue sweater (shit-stained) over her head, not stopping to ease it past her chin and nose. I'm nearly losing my temper, only just not. It's on the bathroom floor. I wipe it off with toilet paper. Mum grabs at me with shitty hands. "Sit down," I say, "stand up. Hold the taps. Oh come on, Mum." I'm being unkind. I rub her with a flannel and she gazes at me in surprise, but doesn't comment. She usually does that bit herself.

I forgot about the Fybogel yesterday morning, but remembered today. Should have anticipated this. Wash pants etc in cold water, because hot will fix the shit. Settle Mum in front of the TV, to watch a western.

She looks at me desolately. Her eyes are swollen. She says "Something's happened to me. I can't do anything." I stroke the hair back from her forehead. "I love you," she says.

"I love you, too. Are you feeling sad?"

"I don't know, Mum," she says.

The wisteria tendrils curl around each other when there's nothing else. Grip and strangle. It pushes in at Mum's window. It goes up behind the window frame and when I pull it out, the tendrils are pale and light-starved, it's been growing in darkness. I remind myself, don't let it get a hold.

"Is it you, Mum? Is it you?" – she questions me. Her bed is soaked. Strip the top sheet, duvet cover, pillow cases, mattress protector and the plastic undersheet. Kennedy women don't cry, if they did they'd be crying all the time, I read that 40 years ago, in a colour supplement. The Kennedys had a better image then. Caroline Bessette-Kennedy, younger generation, same old. Her husband insisted on flying his light aircraft, despite terrible weather conditions. Fathoms deep she sits, the diver reported. No tears. Brave girl.

Perched on the side of the bath, waiting for her – she's on the toilet. Her eyes are shallow as rock pools. Dark lumps of anemone, waiting for the tide, to flower and branch. Oyster shells glisten on the rock, mother of pearl. Sea lavender, bladder campion. It creeps through my veins, the empty and full spaces, it gropes blindly. Death or life? "Are we going to the wild wood?" she asks me.

"Where is the wild wood?"

"I've no idea."

❦

Diazepam's a white pill, the antidepressants are pink. They're big, Diazepam's tiny. I just hope it works. Hey, who's this? A queen enters, crowned with drooping leaves, carrying a broken-backed harp. She looks ill, or worse, under her make-up – a slash of poppy-red lipstick, eyes of a sad clown.

I can hear Mum talking to herself in her bedroom. "Now that is something to do with my complete old children. I give them sweets and apples..."

"Who are you?" I ask the clown queen.

"Diazepam," she says in a sweet young voice. "I can rid you of anxiety. For a while." She swoops at me, a hunting owl, and we kiss. Her breath tastes like being in hospital.

❦

I wake at either 1.30 or 3.30, then I can't get back to sleep. Dr Singh said if you can't sleep, get up and do something. I lie in the darkness, trying to keep my thoughts somewhere elsewhere, lifted off my mind. They always find a way down and in. One thought, then another and another. Hounds attacking.

5.30, wake Mum for a toilet visit. She carpet-skates along the landing. "Yes, I'll just pop to the toilet. Thank you Mum."

Being a carer combines quite well with having a depression/breakdown. One can be fitted in around the other. Except it's often difficult to concentrate. Bedtime's the best time, she's so sweet and funny, laughing. As I'm taking off her clothes – "I shall soon be sitting up here looking like a washing machine. Yes, that's exactly what I shall be doing. I feel quite proud of myself. Darling, you've very lucky to have me."

❦

My brother Mike said he was relieved I'd survived the festive period. "To be honest, I didn't know what I'd find when I got back." What might he have found, in his or my or somebody's worse imaginings? A shrieking madwoman, a fury, a corpse? Keith at the appraisal session said most of my details would be covered by the data protection act, but "of course if you were to tell me you were planning to do something very dreadful…"

Mike said if I'm having suicidal thoughts they might have to remove me from the situation and arrange for me to go into a place where I'd be looked after, cared for. I said, you mean a hospital? He said yes.

Heavy planes are going over, like mechanical sharks, loaded with people. They always follow the same diagonal line. Down here, me and Mum – but for how long and what happens after?

Fear is the concentration of energy in an undesirable form. Fear knocks at the door. Fear takes me by the hand. Muslin fraying into holes around iron corners.

You look exactly the same, they insist. I don't though. I can see my face in the mirror, better than anyone else can see it. An old crumbling brick wall, destroyed by ivy. A garden overrun with ground elder, its roots matted and gnarled. The other plants don't look very well. Instances of joyful upspringing life are becoming rare. Behind the garden stands a once lovely and finely proportioned house, now fallen into decay and ruin. Wet rot, dry rot. Holes in the roof.

Dr Battacharya said, family members often think it started with some or other physical illness, but cast your mind back further, you may recall previous signs of her deterioration.

I change Mum into her nightie, before going to yoga.

"Here's your fleecy top," I say – she likes the word fleecy – "and where are your fleecy socks?" Her fleecy top has a broken zip. Now she's all in blue, celestial.

Laughing, she says "I feel like someone who's just gone to sleep."

In the chemist a woman was talking to her grown-up son, she said "I've cried so many tears, I've got none left to cry."

"Look, Mum" – he pointed to photos of cats advertising Kodak film – "that one's like Archie."

I gave the pharmacist's assistant my prescription and said it was for me. She beckoned me to the other end of the counter and advised keeping a journal. "Your own book. For nobody else but you." She said I could always come into the pharmacy if I needed to talk and she would listen. "We are here for you as well as for your mum." She's had personal experience of depression.

Each plane cuts a wound through sky and pieces of outer space dribble through the holes. Outer space is thirsty for air and so these dark bits inhale vital oxygen, before scurrying back up into the mother ether. The world's healing sustenance is thereby depleted. We become poorer, wronged, estranged. That's why, I think, I'm feeling this way. But I won't go on about it.

One tiny bit of inquisitive darkness, 'conducting research', it told itself, but really just a *flaneur* revelling in absurdity – the world as bouncy castle – this fleck of antimatter was lured into my brain, through my right ear. Then (unfortunately for it and me) all exits and entrances slammed shut and were automatically locked. Whereupon the flibbertigibbety bit of nothingness grew very anxious. I could feel it running back and forth, trapped in the little low space under my skull. It was now a creature, creaturely. Paws and whiskers.

I've been host to it, jailor to it, since last October. Friends and counsellors advise me to be gentle and maybe play it some soothing music. But, but, but, I think. Each time I hurt the mouse, or is it a rat. But my head can't stop thinking but. Last weekend, because of a friend's kindness, my heart sent signals to my brain, which pulled a release lever. The rat or mouse crept mistrustfully through a widening passage into a sunlit cave. It poked around a bit, then sat cleaning its whiskers. This was a much nicer place to be than inside the brain. It even felt safe (sort of, for the time being).

My mother stares me in the face. Her eyes are desperate, haunted. They are angry and hurt. She won't ever get over this. Having to be looked after and told what to do – "I'm being treated like a child," she used to complain. Now she says "I haven't got any children." She accuses the agency carers, "You've taken all my children away." Me, I'm her child, I'm supposed to be looking after her. My spirit in a tortured whirl. Being poked by devils with sharp sticks. Weapons of anguish. Memories.

I'm plodding up the down escalator, carrying – my blanket and hot water bottle my mugs of fruit tea and coffee, my beauty creams, my eyelid hygiene equipment. The escalator keeps going down and down. Up top it's foggy. Across the metal divide, I see Mum. She's naked and clutching just two photos of little girls. Her escalator's going up into celestial light.

A saucer falls out of the kitchen cupboard and cracks, so now it's useless and she throws it in the bin. It's New Year's Day, a terrible omen for the year ahead. She believes in omens, in signs and portents. Maybe cognitive therapy can help her not to. Dr Crowe's referred her to the Tasha Foundation, in the same complex as Age Concern and the Alzheimer's Society. That was weeks ago. They haven't been in touch yet. She follows a ramped concrete path around the building.

A lamb runs in terror from the sunlit field into the dark woods. Then stops, uncertain. It's run a long way into the woods. It's lost. Whatever was scary in the daylight – a shadow, a noise? – now there's really cause for fear. The lamb's ears twitch, its eyes roll back, it bleats. Blehhh! She presses a buzzer. The intercom crackles, hello? She's let in. The reception room or meeting space is vast and gloomy, with pigeonholes. A very young woman takes down her name, doctor's name, contact number, then says she'll ask, disappears, comes back with an appointment time for an initial assessment, 3.45 on Tuesday. Around when the minibus returns from the day centre. "I can't do that, because my mum..." Does she want to reschedule? "Yes please." No other times are available, the girl returns to say. "Oh, OK then."

What are the lamb's chances of survival? Not very high. Is a deep, dark wood a safe place for a lamb or anyone to be lost in?

Mum cries, "There's no hope for us, Mum." She says "I tried to be a reasonable mother."

She has nowhere to go. She doesn't know what to do next. She keeps changing her mind. She feels desperate. She wants to change the past, not to face what might be about to happen. She can't eat. She's jerked awake by nightmarish things she can't remember. She's forgotten how to love, or sit still. She's lost a lot of money. And all her freshness, beauty. She blames the disinfectant. It probably wasn't, though. She keeps looking in the mirror. She makes herself walk briskly twice a day. She's jealous of other people's lives. She can't bear this for one more moment, one more moment.

My brother helps me to move the furniture. I've been sleeping in the little room and Mum in the big room; now Mum will be little, me big. I need more space for my untidiness, also maybe I'll feel better, less cramped, less ill, in this room with its two windows overlooking the street. To my surprise, Lou and Mike have readily acquiesced. But the change might confuse Mum. We'll see.

I swap the clothes contents of two chests-of-drawers, keeping the spare blankets in the lower drawer of the huge chest with its deeply curlicued edges. My head used to fit into that carved space. How could the rest of me have wriggled in underneath? Maybe it wasn't that chest.

The little room is transformed into something so beautiful and exactly right-seeming, I want to move straight back in there. Mum's creamy-buff bed against the light wall, a Victorian fireplace, an elegant chair. The big room just looks messy now. Faded, dirty yellow-and-white striped wallpaper. Mike says, hand on chin, "You could do a lot with this room."

Downstairs – "It's the depression, it's not you. There's Frances and then there's the depression." Mike talks of depression goggles, of clouds moving over the sunlit fields. "Ask her" – he points at Mum. "She knows."

Mum looks at me, sad-eyed. "I know."

It's hard to stop yourself from peering anxiously in the mirror. Helen says you look exactly the same, Mike says all depressed people look awful. It's like that Stephen King film, except you're the evil hotel room, your own maelstrom of devils, ghosts and nightmares. Gemma says disapprovingly, so your doctor just keeps handing out sick notes? Mum's crying on the toilet, she says "Never mind Mum, it's just that I'm sort of bleeding at the moment."

She says, "I love you more than anyone in the world."

❦

The lodestone inside my head has been swinging wildly on its chain, that's why now I can't ever not even for a moment feel peace, balance, gentleness, quiet, gratitude, hope, faith. Because of my shredded inner self and because of the lodestone. Venlafaxine is trying to calm it with magnetic energy, that's a clever idea, but will it work? Will it stop the lodestone from sucking everything into its dark centre?

Yesterday morning she crept in here and wet the bed. The mattress was soaked. I put it out for the special waste collection, luckily one was booked already. I'd been uncertain whether to include the mattress. Order a new bed and – no, just the bed. No just the mattress. I have to think, plan, act. I have to survive. Arrange things, then change my mind. Make appointments, cancel them. Do the paperwork. Tear it up.

Where do I live, exactly? I keep thinking of my last-but-one address. The blackbird singing on the chimney. A rose called Deep Secret. I've gone missing from there. I wonder, do the neighbours miss me? The cats, the birds, the trees? Or have I just closed up and vanished, like a wound healed over?

A bit sort of detached, I told Dr Crowe. She asked, any negative side-effects? Headache, sore throat, feel sick and whenever I close my eyes I see terrible things. A man buried in a pile of corpses. They stick pikes in, trying to finish off anyone who's still alive.

I think if I hadn't talked about my depression it would never have gained power over me. My brother says this is a story, not a fact.

I saw a dark whirling like a swarm of bees only more intense and in a tubular shape. Very complex, inward, rushing around and into itself, deadly. Then I heard a voice,

Mike's – "I need you to write down what you see. Your mind goes into a very dark place sometimes that's close to despair. Remember, though, it's only a story."

Mum comments on the passers-by – "That woman seemed to be carrying a large chicken... He's got an enormous beard. It's awful to wake up in the morning and some-one's got an enormous beard."

I'm thinking about her friends, the ones who persist. Although they're frightened by the changes in her, still they visit, they make determined conversation.

Anyway, she hasn't died. Only brain cells.

"She's not our Mum any more" – my sister. I suppose that's true.

"Smoking!" – Mum points to a pigeon pecking at a cig-arette end. It's missing several toes. Many pigeons have injured feet.

"Are you cold?" I ask her.

Defensively: "Not unless you are."

I retrieve her gloves from her pockets, her scarf from where it's slipped down inside her coat. "Whoops, whoops. Oh dear, I'm a teddy-bear."

My vision clears and there's the most beautiful thing, a huge ash tree. Black buds, green and purple flowers, all springy and alive in the blue sky. "Look, Mum! Look at that tree!" I seize her arm.

"Yes, you're here darling," she says (to me or the tree?). "You're doing your best."

The Estate

The suburban estate was built between two public parks, with shops and schools nearby. Three-bedroom houses on tree-lined, made-up roads, with cavity walls, bay windows, fitted kitchens, garage space. No road or legal charges, said the builder's advertisement. Special features could be ordered, such as cornicing in the hallways, a lamp on the staircase, parquet flooring. The detached houses cost £875, the semis £785.

People moved in and stayed for decades. They raised families, despite the small kitchens, and were grateful to have an indoor bathroom. On Saturdays they went shopping – the women wore long black gloves and stepped into the passenger seats of saloon cars, through doors held open by their husbands.

Extensions were built, attics converted, double glazing installed. Old people died, houses changed hands, the quiet family area with its good primary schools attracted a mix of cultures. The local Methodist church ran an Alpha course, also popular were line-dancing classes and the Over 50s club. New developments clustered around the tube station. The greengrocer, the butcher and the paint and hardware shop all closed and were replaced by charity outlets; people shopped at the big Asda, or at Marks & Spencer Simply Food. The century turned.

By now, foxes had become a problem. Killing them was illegal, but some people hid poison in the black plastic bin bags. Put out on Sunday nights with the recycling bins, to be collected on Monday mornings, the bags were often torn open, littering the street. The council introduced a new bin system.

War came, then plague. Huge rats. A hail of dust. Most people died quickly. At last, everyone was dead.

An orange moon. Shrieks in the wind. Broken gutters, smashed windows, doors hanging off their hinges, torn-up floorboards.

No more original features or new things, no schools, shops, TVs, computers, no electricity or gas, no piped water, no comforts of life, no human life. Soon the houses will be gone, the estate a wasteland.

Another turn of the century, this time nobody is keeping count.

The Golden Hour

That afternoon was a particularly trying one for Mary. Having changed her mother's incontinence pad and left her on the sofa watching *Homes under the Hammer*, she had retreated upstairs, planning to work. But after turning on her computer, she heard the rattle and scrape of a metal stepladder being positioned outside, on the dank strip of gravel between the privet hedge and the bay. Its treads squeaked under the awkward weight of someone not expert at climbing ladders, but determined to ascend.

Sonia from number six then appeared at eye level, wearing an apron over her dress and brandishing a pair of secateurs. As usual she was fully made up, her lipstick coral-coloured, her bright brown eyes heavily mascara-ed.

Mary reluctantly got to her feet, twiddled open a brass security lock and eased up the sash window. "Hello?" she said.

"I've come to prune the wisteria, which is something I do regularly," Sonia informed her. "Otherwise your mother's house would just disappear. Wisteria is a terrible plant, it gets everywhere. Strangles your brickwork and if you don't mind me saying so, it brings the whole neighbourhood down."

"I've always thought it rather pretty," Mary said, looking with regret at the heavy panicles of flowers, now in green bud tinged with mauve. She supposed this draped abundance did look a bit out of place in a narrow street of plain Victorian houses. Though not half as odd as number 31, now reconstructed in the style of a half-timbered Tudor mansion and sticking out awkwardly in the long terrace.

"Only for two weeks a year," Sonia replied sharply. "It's got a short flowering season. Anyway, I prune it for your mother, to save her the trouble."

"That's very kind of you." Mary wanted to ask Sonia to come back another time, or go away altogether, but instead asked "Would you like a cup of tea?"

"Yes, when I'm finished. Of course now you're living here, you could do it yourself."

"Perhaps I could," Mary said guardedly.

"Don't you go out to work?" Sonia jabbed the secateurs at Mary's chin.

Mary flinched and withdrew into the room. She had no wish to offend, but also would rather not join a six-hour queue in Accident and Emergency. "No, I work from home, editing academic texts."

"That's nice. So you don't have to risk being blown up by terrorists. Like my sister."

"Your sister?" Mary said, rather startled.

"She's an office worker. Has to travel in and out by tube."

"Oh, I see."

"Anyway" – Sonia abruptly changed the subject – "You need to get those gutters cleared. Or they'll overflow and then you'll have terrible problems. People often do ignore their gutters, until the rain comes creeping indoors. And by then it's too late." Her tone implied horrors beyond Mary's capacity to imagine. "The insurers won't pay up, either. Tell you what, if you like I'll ring someone. They might be able to come round this afternoon, with proper ladders. I can't reach that high on just a stepladder," she said aggressively, as though Mary had suggested she might. "It wouldn't be safe."

"I'll just go and see to my mother," Mary desperately excused herself and hurried from the room, in what she felt was a cowardly retreat, but really the only option left to her. Her instinct was always to placate, or scuttle off. As she went downstairs, she reflected not for the first time that living here put her in an invidious position, at the mercy of all callers and their opinions. Partly belonging, but without rights of retreat and self-protection. Her mother's home was not Mary's castle.

She remembered how, many years ago, she'd watched from her back bedroom window as the girl from upstairs, kneeling on the patio, determinedly scraped moss from the bricks around the drain. She had no business being there at all, since the garden was for Mary's sole use. But Mary had simply moved away from the window, out of sight. If she ventured outside to protest, she knew who would get the worst of it. She did not want to be lectured on the disgraceful state of her own outside wall.

Ros had fallen asleep on the sofa, oblivious to little bursts of music and excited commentary. Her scalp was pink under thin white hair. Apart from age spots and a few deep wrinkles her skin was clear, her face free of sorrow and anxiety.

Mary switched off the TV and looked down at her mother. It was almost possible to believe she would wake up quite well again, as the loving and concerned mum, the intelligent, lucid person she had been. The woman who had once ruthlessly captured an escaped geriatric wandering along the pavement in her nightgown, trapped her with false assurances and driven her straight back to the local care home. For each man in his time plays many parts, Mary thought. Time wreaks its hideous but natural changes. Experience is lost, innocence regained.

Ros's eyelids flickered and she began to twitch and make whimpering noises. Then she woke up. "Are we all packed and ready to go?" she asked. "Will we be leaving soon? Oh dear, what will happen to us?"

"It's OK, Mum. Everything's all right," Mary said soothingly.

"Grasshoppers are crawling all over the house!" cried Ros. "Help!" She caught sight of the stepladder outside the window and was diverted. "A foot" she said, laughing.

"That's Sonia, Mum. She's pruning the wisteria."

"I don't believe you. Now tell me, how old am I?"

"You're eighty."

"And how old are you?"

"I'm fifty-four."

Ros thought this over, her expression doubtful. "You must have had a child very young, in that case," she said. "Because you were fifty-four when I was just a baby. And then I had several more old children."

"Would you like your supper now?" Mary interrupted her mother's random calculations. "Shall I pop it into the microwave?"

"Pop! Pop!" Ros waved her arms enthusiastically. Mary withdrew to the kitchen, where the rush matting laid down by her mother a decade or so ago to cover the cracked red quarry tiles was now worn and encrusted with dirt. She did some washing up until the microwave beeped. The food was divided into neat plastic compartments – breaded fish, peas, potatoes – and Mary thought it looked quite appetising, as she transferred it to a plate. Wiltshire Farm Foods, delivered in a van to one's door or freezer, and popular with all the old folk. The packs compared well in price to 'meals on wheels', the disgusting council mush. She arranged plate, cutlery, a glass of orange juice and a paper napkin on a tray.

Brushing back through the curtain that divided the kitchen from the main living area, she came face to face with Sonia. "Here you are!" their neighbour exclaimed. "I was worried in case you'd had an accident or something. You were both so quiet, I could only hear the television."

Mary stood still, amazed. Did Sonia know a secret way into her mother's house, she wondered, through some tunnel or hidden door? Having the advantage of height, she could see past Sonia into both sitting room and half-hallway. The front door was standing wide open. Ros had disappeared.

This was impossible, Mary's fogged mind argued. She always kept the front door locked, as her mother was liable to wander. Ros could open doors but not unlock them, although sometimes she poked bits of card or paper into the keyhole and twisted them experimentally.

With trembling hands, she put the tray down on the dining table. "Where is my mother?"

"Oh, she went out," said Sonia. "She rushed past me in just her nightie and a fleece jacket and slippers. I did think it was strange for her not to be wearing proper clothes, in the daytime. Ros should be kept looking nice and fresh, I thought to preserve her dignity. But perhaps I shouldn't criticise. No doubt you think it's none of my business. Your mum left a spare key with me, yonks ago, in case of an emergency. Anyway I just wanted to check with you, before I ring the men to clear your gutters. It'll be about £80. They could do mine as well, while they're about it..."

Leaving Sonia to ramble on – in case of an emergency? This was an emergency! – Mary ran outside, up the road, in one direction then another. "Mum! Mum!" she screamed. She came to the McDonald's and a dual carriageway with two sets of traffic lights. Surely her mother couldn't have crossed here? Holding a stitch in her side, Mary looked down over the children's playground, the river path, the shiny and swirling Thames. I must ring the police, she thought.

Two policemen arrived at the house, their shoes squeaking on the lush carpet of massacred wisteria. They insisted on searching upstairs, then asked Mary to unlock the back door. "She can't possibly be out there!" Mary protested.

As they patrolled the 20ft garden, she realised they were checking for freshly turned earth, signs of recent burial. She hoped they wouldn't disturb the fox, whose den was under the lilac bush. But really, this was ridiculous! They were losing time, she agitated.

"Sorry, but there are some very strange people around," the senior officer told her, re-entering the kitchen and stamping on a non-existent doormat. Poor old bird, she could see him thinking, observing her stressed face and untidy hair. Having a breakdown, maybe? Spinster, carer, no real life of her own. She'd been pruning her wisteria at totally the wrong time of year, it should be done in winter. And clearly no one ever gardened out the back.

The two officers' expressions were no longer mistrustful and Mary noted hopefully that two-way radios were being used.

"OK. Now we swing into action," the senior one announced.

"Good," Mary said, controlling her voice. "Thank you."

"Shops and supermarkets are often good points of call, so we'll ask there after we've knocked on your neighbours' doors. Have you got a picture of her?"

After a rummage, Mary produced a blurred group photo, her mother hemmed in by a group of smiling relatives. Underneath it in the drawer was the profile portrait of a glamorous young actress. Oh Mum, how beautiful you were. "This one shows her nose better. But of course she was much younger..."

"The more recent one, please."

Mary sat crying in the window seat, in full view of anyone walking past, but not caring. Mum, Mum, where are you? It was getting dark. Several neighbours had expressed concern and were searching in their cars. A lost child was most likely to be found in the first hour, the officer had told her. The golden hour, he'd called it. "And with respect, your mother is like a child." Yes, she was pleased he'd grasped that. But now at least three hours had gone by, with no sign of Ros.

There are some very strange people around, he'd said... Might there be people who seized lost old ladies, kidnapped them from the streets and tortured them? But surely, surely, others would be kind.

To whom apart from herself would her mother be of any value? Though she was loved and so sweet, with her odd and charming phrases. "He hedgehogged off," she remembered Ros saying last week, after they'd watched a hedgehog amble into the dusk. Oh Mum...

Bedtime came and went; Mary kept vigil at the window. No news, although the police had returned twice to update her on their lack of progress. People across the road switched off their lights, first downstairs then upstairs.

She couldn't even lie down on the sofa and rest for a few moments, in case her mother turned up. But what if Ros never turned up – had vanished altogether and permanently? Then it seemed to Mary she would never be able to sleep again.

She thought momentarily of Sonia, who had not offered to help with the search. Guilty conscience? That was probably too much to hope for.

At 11.40pm, she went to the kitchen to make herself coffee. The doorbell rang.

Mary hastened to open the door and there stood Ros. A tartan blanket was pinned around her shoulders, over her nightgown; it made her look quite dashing and handsome. Her pink slippers were exceedingly grubby. Her legs were bruised.

"Mum!" As Mary ushered her mother indoors, a car started in the road. A woman waved from its dark interior.

The car turned the corner and was gone.

"Here you are," Ros greeted her. "Where have you *been*?"

"Oh Mum. Where have *you* been?"

"I fell on the railway. Some men drinking at tables told me no, no, no. Then she said to her husband, I'll take the car."

"So you remembered your address?" Mary said in astonishment.

"I certainly did. Up the ivy runs the weasel, to midnight road, a cul de sac with balloons on sticks," Ros gibbered. She was hyper. Well, maybe the kind stranger would return at some point to get her tartan blanket.

"Come on, Mum. Let's get you to bed..." Mary propelled Ros up the stairs. And if not, she thought, the blanket would make a nice throw for the sofa.

Had a Heart

When I was a child and then a young girl, I had emotional problems. I lacked feelings. The world seemed dead to me. Our GP couldn't help, so my mum took me to see a specialist, Dr Cheddar-Mouse (his name sounded like that, anyway). He said I needed an extra heart and luckily he could get hold of one by the following Tuesday.

"Will she have to have an operation?" my mum asked.

Dr Cheddar-Mouse kept glancing at the sky through his surgery window. His mind was up there among the fast-blowing clouds. However, he reassured us: no operation. And he gave me a pink felt-tip pen that smelled of roses.

A flesh-and-blood heart looks like something from the butcher's, whereas a metaphorical heart sparkles with radiant light. It wasn't easy to swallow, but I did. "Well done, good girl," said the doctor. Then it was inside my chest. I felt like Jesus, astonishing. "The illumination will gradually fade."

Joys and sorrows! Fire and floods! New world!

I grew up and met my husband, Jim. Of course I told him about my two hearts, but he only laughed disbelievingly. My chest ached, eyes filled, and he accused me of being "too sensitive", a familiar comment. I wrote a poem about it, my usual way of coping, and soon had enough material for a third slim volume.

However, I failed to keep a finger on the pulse of my marriage. Soon a dislike grew between us, a malevolence. Quarrels erupted. One of these started in the house but soon we were on the heath, flinging bitter accusations as we strode along. A man was flying a kite and I recognised him, just as our disagreement reached a crisis of horribleness. I bent over, choking and retching. Somebody hit me from behind, and there was my heart lying in the grass. "Well done, good girl," the doctor said. "Better out than in."

He'd managed to keep the kite flying, although it was a two-hander – a multi-coloured bird with a diamond-shaped tail. "That's a nice kite," I said, already noticing a difference, since nice hadn't previously been a word in my vocabulary. My husband continued raging, but now I found it easy to shut up. Back home, I put the heart in my bedside drawer.

In my new calmer state, I began noticing things. Like, Jim wasn't around much. Then I overheard sobs in the bathroom. A week or so later, I thought to check on my heart.

But when I opened the drawer, it was gone.

He's never denied that he took my heart and gave it to his lukewarm lady love. I don't know how he tricked her into swallowing it. Maybe concealed in a bun.

Anyway, Dr Cheddar-Mouse tells me I don't need it, because my system has adjusted. I spend my days on the heath, you might think peacefully but no, the kite world is fraught with emotional drama.

Our Family Life as Orphans and Thieves

About half-way through last Wednesday, my brother A drove us north to Loose Chippings to visit Aunt Daisy. A has eyes in the back of his head, quite an unnerving feature in a driver. But he has eyes in front too and these were fixed on the road. Also crammed into A's Vauxhall Viva (which is older than any of us) were my younger brother B and the twins, I and W. And me of course, M, though luckily I don't take up much space.

Aunt D's house is gloomily extensive. Hidden here, we suspect, are cousins in dozens and possibly one or two ex-spouses. For instance, if you pass too close to a wall, often something you might have taken for a bit of rough plastering or lumpy wallpaper will detach itself, apologise and scurry away. The front outlook is of a greasy sort of field. Nobody ever looks out the back, for obvious reasons.

Our aunt confounds the saying fresh-as-a-daisy, for she is wizened and smells off. Rusty stains marked the bibbed front of her old-fashioned dress. We mumbled our appreciation of the tea table she'd laid for our visit: stale biscuits doubling as drinks coasters, marshmallows like pillows for bad dreams, and portions of burnt cabbage. After some initial pleasantries, the real conversation – the one we'd hoped to avoid – began.

"But isn't burglary a crime, I mean in the eyes of the law?" A pleaded.

"It would be criminal not to put your talents and abilities to good use," Aunt D replied. "Has nobody ever yet realised your joint potential? I find that extraordinary. And yet so typical. For you" – she fixed on me and my always unreliable stomach went helter skelter – "are a small man with a smaller vocation. You two, I and W, are pale angels. B, you drive the only train to nowhere island. And A, A, you're a bit scary." I think she meant all these remarks as encomiums, but we did not feel very flattered.

"Typical?" A queried, referring back a few sentences.

"Of your mother. She never noticed anything."

B spoke gruffly: "But we've survived so far." His meaning was unclear to us all.

"And I expect great things of you in the very near future!" Aunt Daisy shooed us out of her front door in a bustling and merry way, like an entirely fictional aunt.

Shivering in colloquy, we had the idea of a trial run, a practice effort. Of going round to the back of Auntie D's own house and breaking into one of her forbidden rooms. This may be what she'd intended us to do all along, I don't know.

B ratcheted himself up. Pressing his side in a place that's known only to him and a few close relatives – but it's where a saint may have the stigmata – he extended bodily till he was gazing down at us from where a window might be, only wasn't yet. I then laddered up him. Crooned to the wall and touched it gently. Became its lover, uttering vows and deceitful promises. Lightly traced a square. And the wall fell, as walls will do – or at least, an opening appeared. Glass shimmered cleanly in two overlapping white frames. I pushed up the window and so we entered. A helped me jump from the sill, then B clambered over it.

The window became disillusioned and vanished; we felt for each other in the dark. I shunned I's touch. In my opinion it is wrong to take selfish advantage of the love of innocent things, especially those called into being through your own treacherous behaviour. Although, of course, I myself had benefited from the window's exploitation, I was guilty too, and perhaps that's why I felt so cross with I. But really, he lacks all conscience and heart.

To judge by the smell and general atmosphere, we'd entered a room seldom if ever used. In the musty enclosed darkness we stood together, breathing. Or rather it did, the family creature. Severely damaged, yet alive and thoughtful. Remembering the person our mother used to be. The dementia was partly a blessing, since by the time she died she was lost to us already, a beautiful shell. And we'd grown up. Only our physical selves and weird proclivities now signify the love that afflicted us once.

We heard I murmuring enticements, followed by a scuffle as W slapped him away from the wall. "There's a perfectly good switch here already," she said. "Voilà!" A dingy light bloomed.

We were standing in a laboratory. Floorboards, cupboards. Body fragments in jars on shelves, pickled but not recently I opined, since the fluid was cloudy. "Oh my," A said. He unscrewed a jar and extracted a hand. A lady's.

B launched into an old song, one of our mother's and poignant for that reason. His fine baritone reverberated in the dusty air. "Nothing else would matter in the world today, we could go on living in the same old way…" But could we? With Mum gone, did we even have that option?

A put the hand in his pocket – our first act of thievery. Then he tried and failed to open the door. "We'll have to break it."

"No we won't," said W. "There's the key." She pointed to a black iron key, on a ledge above a rusty storage heater. "Locked from the inside. Unless Auntie has a spare."

"Ah."

We recombined and cautiously ventured out. A number of corridors with associated flights of stairs and half landings took us nowhere in particular. In the course of our journeying we ignored many other rooms. Their ghastly secrets were probably irrelevant, surplus to requirements or at least too much for us to absorb and benefit from right now.

Besides, things of their nature remain mysterious. Such as, why did our mother pour orange juice into the cat's dish? Often I was just too late to prevent her, running on my short legs – "Mum, no!" Her old cat, also called A, would pad forward to investigate, then turn away in disgust. Brown cubes floating in an orange sea.

"Don't stop me," W said, and for a moment, owing to the muddle of recollection, I thought she was Mum. But no. We'd come to the head of a staircase like a well, or some other receptacle of darkness. Stairs that clearly required a human sacrifice. And with hardly a pause W, vanquished by an urgency that's both ancient and personal, threw herself down them. She was gone.

"Jesus," said A. "That's all we need."

Gazing dolefully from the banisters, we recalled peering into an open grave in an eastern cemetery while trying to attend our mother's funeral. A new coffin with a shiny plaque lay in the clay-streaked hole, but A with his sharpest pair of eyes discerned it wasn't hers, nor that of our father. At the same time he espied the correct hearse, far away. We hurried after it, A ferrying me on his shoulders, but alas, we missed the committal ceremony.

Too late again. So much always depends on timing.

"There's a chance," B said in a level voice, "that she won't quite have managed to kill herself."

We exchanged horrified glances. "She's never botched the job yet," A calmly and reasonably pointed out.

Nor had she this time. The staircase was a long one – unfeasibly so, given the height of Aunt Daisy's house – and a bit clingy, but not the very worst type of stairs, because eventually we reached the ground floor. And there lay our sister. Dead.

Yes, dead. We knelt beside her. B clasped her small, limp arm gently between his two fists the size of boulders. I's high keening noise was like a cat about to attack another cat. The scene brought to mind our mother's quiet decease, witnessed only by a stranger, our other brother. A's Vauxhall Viva was stuck in traffic at the time. It seemed so unfair. But as Mum herself would have replied, life isn't fair either.

We were kneeling in a snowy waste, divided from the sky by dark woods. The snow was obviously either an illusion or a symbol, yet it kept falling. And we kept brushing it from W's face, to prevent her features from becoming obscured. As though we feared – what? That she might turn into someone else?

I thought the snow was like the frozen tears we hadn't yet managed to cry. Perhaps because we didn't really believe or accept that Mum had died.

"We need to make sacrifices," A said. At that moment, a louse fell from his hair on to W's forehead. "A volunteer. Splendid." He cracked it between finger and thumb. The corpse took a breath and became a shade less pale.

A rummaged in the deep pockets of his dungarees and brought out the stolen lady's hand, it looked arthritic in the bluey snowlight. Having considered it for a moment, he put it back. Next he found one of Aunt Daisy's homemade buns, saved from the terrible tea table, "just in case I might need to poison something," A explained, tearing it apart.

A squirrel ran towards us from the dark woods and

grabbed a piece. Never made it back home. The corpse's eyelids flickered, dreaming. Rooks cawed, as though we'd disturbed the peace of the woods, and flew above our heads. I pointed; one fell, its blood spattering the snow.

W sat up. "Urgh, I've got a headache. I'll never do that again." And we believed her. Which is to say, she believed herself. "It's cold," she added.

This was her first resurrection since Mum's death, which made it seem quite special.

We are a greatly gifted family, apart from me. A small man with a smaller vocation, to quote Aunt Daisy. But perhaps it's a mistake to think of myself as an individual, a separate person, a 'family member'. Rather, we are like bees – all parts of a macro-organism, interdependent on the other parts. And therefore the single bee need not berate itself with regard to its honey-gathering or other capacities. Indeed since the bee mind is communal, the single bee does not exist. I took off my cable-knit jumper and draped it around W's shoulders. At least it would help to warm part of her back. "Thank you, sweet M."

The snow had begun to thaw. We followed the direction of I's eyes, since he is a natural compass, though not a moral one, and found ourselves amid the dripping trees. It was Spring. The earth smelled of bitter moss. "Listen," B said, "I've got early-stage what Mum had. My brain is full of holes. Enough to comprehend suspenseful aspects of the infinite. So given a cornfield and a clear blue sky, I might climb into emptiness. Perhaps we should take advantage of the facility and just all disappear."

"Yes," I said. "I'm game."

A took the lady's hand from his pocket and kissed it reverently, then scraped a hole in the leaf mould and buried it. Saying farewell to all earthly loves and desires. But his Yes lacked conviction. I suspect his destiny is to be a loving husband and father.

I, standing very close to W, smiled as though he'd already passed into bliss. "Yes," he said. Which meant nothing.

Drips fell. Small birds sang. The buried hand grew into a tree, leafed and blossomed with hands in plenty. At last – "No," said W. And her no overcame our yes. Or rather, it was a true Yes.

"We owe it to our brother," she said, "not to grieve him without cause." I must say this surprised me. I thought it showed a very mature attitude.

The lady tree waved a many-handed goodbye as we trudged off. Before long we came to the edge of the woods and saw Aunt D's house across a field, with the Vauxhall Viva parked outside.

We bundled into the car and A released the handbrake without turning on the engine. Silently we coasted, stole ourselves away. Escaped.

As we sped along the dual carriageway, I gazed from a side window, feeling melancholy. To be small often just seems like nothing. Or close to nothing. Or not close enough. Once I wrote to the world's smallest man, to ask his advice. He said he'd often felt quite low too, until he was declared the smallest man in the world, but now he views his lack of height as a positive asset. He also thanked me for writing and mentioned that he prefers letters to emails.

Mrs Honeywell's Dance

The Honeywells' Spring Cocktail Party is normally un-eventful – drinks and nibbles, neighbourly chit-chat. But last year, Mrs Honeywell took us all by surprise. Having turned up the music, she began to dance in the manner of Salomé, removing items of clothing and dropping them on the Axminster carpet. We quickly made space. Mrs Honeywell's toned and tanned figure, her large white breasts, the bold elegance of her dancing style, impressed us. Then, slipping through the curtains, she vaulted over a balcony rail and escaped into the dusk. Honeywell re-entered the room; we praised his wife's performance. Eh, he said, what?

Where Are We Now?

My mother asks me this question repeatedly. Where are we now? She seldom asks who I am, or who she is. The where is what puzzles her.

Where are we now? In your house, Mum. In London, sort of, cramped between the North Circular and the Great West Road. In a life crisis, a breakdown. And in early-stage Alzheimer's, becoming advanced.

Where are we now? I wish she wouldn't keep asking this same question, making this identical demand. It's like being pestered by a small child, interrogated by the enemy. I try to answer honestly while varying my responses.

She's crying on the toilet. "What's happening to me?"

I hold her hand. "Do you mean today?"

"No, I don't mean today."

"Or more generally speaking?"

"Yes," she says. "I mean generally speaking."

I say, you've got dementia, but it's OK, there are still lots of lovely things about you and you have children and grandchildren.

Children and grandchildren, how trite. She might as well have no one. She's lying down now, for a rest.

Where are we now? In Mum's tiny garden, which I suppose is now my garden too. It's overhung by next door's massive eucalyptus, which sucks all the moisture from the soil. Only a few years ago, this tree greatly preoccupied my mother. If woman ever hated tree, she hated this one. But now it might as well not exist, for all the attention she pays it. And the fox that sleeps in the dry flowerbed has made itself scarce. While the cat is here, but dead. I've dug a hole by the jasmine-laden fence, to bury her in. A thin old cat with skin-diseased fur. Bare around her neck where the collar rubbed her, before I noticed and took it off. Life damages us, but if that's not OK, at least death makes it of no matter finally. Mum sits peacefully on her mould-spotted bench. Once I've filled in the hole, I lay a piece of trellis over it and weight that down with a heavy pot, in case the fox tries to unearth her.

Where are we now? In the West Middlesex hospital. "People have a lot of thoughts in their heads," Mum says.

"I expect you have a lot of thoughts in your head, too."

"Not a lot."

Lilian in the next bed is complaining to her daughter-in-law about Mum getting special treatment. She is fed by hand, while Lilian has to feed herself.

"We're going to buy you a new carpet," her daughter-in-law changes the subject. "and paint your flat, it will all be ready by the time you get home."

"You say so," Lilian replies.

"What kind of carpet would you like?"

"Green" says Lilian. "Squares. No rough patterns."

The daughter-in-law looks taken aback. "OK. Well we'll see about the squares. We'll see about the colour."

"Love you, darling," Mum tells me as I'm going. "Love you lots. I adore you, actually."

Where are we now? In a residential home. The agency carer once told me, it would kill your mum to go into a home. And now, where are we? In the lounge. Many bad legs – rotting, bruised. Letty shouts from her corner table, "She's a snob!" – Mum, she means. "She won't talk to us."

I start to explain, but Letty interrupts. "I like *you*," she says. "You're not a snob." Then she burps. Letty's burps get on my brother's nerves, he's told me. I know what he means, but she obviously enjoys burping. It's self-expression of a kind.

As I'm hurrying along the pavement a few days later, my nose shines at me from DrugSaver's window. Forgot to put on make-up. Rummage in my bag, find nothing. I'll have to visit Mum with a shiny nose. This will be OK if nobody notices, i.e. if Mani isn't one of the care staff on duty. She always comments on my appearance. Now I'm in DrugSaver. I'm reluctant to spend more than £10 on a mirror compact of powder, but I can't find any sample pots. Sneakily I take a compact from the display rack, open it and dab powder on my nose. It's orange. I look ridiculous. Worse, a member of staff instantly spots me (I'm the only customer in the store), furiously rebukes me – "We can't sell it now you've used it!" – and insists I pay at the till. Where they keep me waiting. I'm in disgrace, an attempted powder thief. They probably have CCTV footage of my orange nose.

As soon as a care assistant has noticed me waving frantically in the home's glass porch and tapped in the code to let me through, I scuttle to the nearest toilet. Here among the hoists and spare wheelchairs, I first try to wash the powder off my nose – the scarlet-orange nose of distress and embarrassment – then re-cover the nose and my entire face. To 'blend in', which it doesn't, but I give up. It's better than nothing. Probably.

I can't find Mum anywhere in the lounge. Then I do.

Someone's apparently poured boiling water over her head, or set fire to her. The left side of her face and scalp is all red and blistered. Mum, I say, Mum. She hisses through her teeth. What's happened to you? Hiss, hiss, is her only answer.

Mani is spooning medicine into Paulette's open mouth. I interrupt: "Do you know..."

She looks up in surprise, then bursts out laughing. "What's happened to *you*?"

Back home, I phone my sister. She's good at sorting things out and confronting people. All guns blazing, that's her style of going in. Oh yes, she says, the home rang me yesterday about a rash on Mum's face.

"It's more like burns than a rash. And she's in pain, I'm sure she is." I'd tried to get help, but the office was closed. Mum's face looked better today than yesterday, according to Mani. "If it looked worse yesterday, I'm surprised they didn't call an ambulance."

"OK, hold on," Zoe says. "I'll ring them on my mobile."

To entertain me while I'm waiting, her son Abe tells me a joke. "Knock knock," he says.

"Who's there?"

"Control freak. Now *you* say, control freak who?"

"Control freak who?"

"No, stupid. That's the joke."

My sister in the background: "Don't be rude."

"Oh sorry, I see. Ha ha!"

Zoe returns. "Apparently they did call the GP and he prescribed an antibiotic. He thinks it'll clear up in a couple of days. He doesn't know exactly what..."

"She looks terrible!"

"OK. Leave it with me."

Zoe contacts her nurse friend Liz, who kindly pops in to visit Mum and diagnoses shingles. The GP agrees that's probably what it is and changes his prescription. Mum's face heals quickly and soon she only has a few scabby bits left.

Whenever I visit the home, Mum's sitting with her eyes closed. She is far away. Lost in thoughts or memories, or perhaps she's given her tangled and befuddled mind the slip, escaped into some larger freedom. Winging on emptiness, like a seagull riding the air currents. She will find a sort of happiness in it, the psychic told me.

Mum, Mum, I say. Her eyes open. She pretends to recognise me. I'm sorry to have called her back, from wherever she was.

Where are we now? Trying to find my dad's grave, on Mum's burial day. Since he was interred a quarter century ago I've never visited him, so I've forgotten where the grave is. Also the cemetery is vast. I'm here with my new love and we've arrived far too early. I think my sister said to gather at the main gates, so for a while we sit on a bench nearby, holding hands and enjoying the mid February sun. Then it occurs to us, we might as well go looking for an open grave, or a hole covered over with green cloth, fake grass, with planks laid on the mud to protect the shiny black shoes of the undertaker's men and women. They're easy to spot. Here's one, a coffin already planted in its depths. I can just make out name and dates on the brass plaque and it's not Mum, definitely. We're laughing now, ha ha!

Here's Janet, a plain-clothed nun, my mum's long-time friend, they met at drama school. Janet's sister Bridget is here too. They know exactly where to go, the old part of the cemetery, higher up. Within its yew hedges, quiet and birdsong. The bearded Unitarian minister – he's a last-minute substitute for the church's usual woman minister, who knew Mum, a pity but it can't be helped – is standing by the grave in his vestments. As we introduce ourselves, my mobile starts to play a merry polka.

It's Zoe. She's at the main gates, everyone else is there too and the hearse has arrived. "Where are you, darling?"

– determinedly patient, as though addressing a child or an idiot.

"We're at the grave. The minister's here too, and Sister Janet." Religious authority is on my side.

"OK, stay there."

I wander around in the grave's vicinity. Dad's headstone has been temporarily uprooted, it's lying flat. Mum thought his name was carved in too-big letters, too near the edges, which upset her. It looks fine to me, though. She made a garden in and around the grave, with lavender etc. Spending a lot of time there, she became part of a little cemetery community. I remember her telling me about the other dead people and their living relatives, one of whom died quite unexpectedly, a young man visiting his dad's grave with his mum. As they waited on seats by the bus stop to go home again, he leaned against his mother and sighed – and he too was gone, his co-ordinates forever lost to her, because wherever people go, they certainly don't stick around in bus shelters or graveyards. They are not laid to rest, they don't RIP, their bodies just become irrelevant. At least that's been my excuse for not visiting Dad.

Also I search for but can't find the stone of a teenage girl who killed herself, recalling its inscription, which Mum told me about:

'Oh for it would be a pity
To o'erpraise her or to flout her.
She was wild and sweet and witty –
Let's not say dull things about her.'

A poet friend disdainfully commented, when I recited this: first you die, then they put bad verse on your tombstone. But Mum and I thought it was lovely.

I can hear the Unitarian minister talking to Janet and Bridget and assuming they're Church of England. Shocked, they chorus "No, we're Catholic!"

The funeral carriage approaches us down a long, wide avenue. And behind... It's like that scene in the two Harvey

Milk films, after he's been shot, when his friends think no-one's bothered to turn up to the vigil. Then looking down from City Hall they see thousands of lights, people holding candles. Well, Mum's procession isn't quite so impressive. But nearly. It may even include Dad's mad cousin Henrietta, who's rung me several times to stress how inconvenient the date is for her.

There's Mum's sister, 90 years old, walking with the rest. And my nephew in a black suit. I wonder if he knows any knock knock jokes about death. Like in the Pardoner's Tale, the old man who goes about tapping the earth, "my moodres gate", with his staff, and crying dear mother let me in. Knock knock. Who's there...

The minister says a few inappropriate words in praise of Unitarianism and Mum is lowered into the grave, in a fabulous bamboo coffin. Right then the clouds part and the sun shines down like a blessing or a reassurance. Zoe grabs me – she remembers the same thing happened at Dad's funeral.

Beckoned forward to the grave's edge, I scatter earth and pass the trowel to Zoe. Then our brother kneels and throws in a single flower.

My Lion

Today I saw my lion. It's been a couple of years since my last appointment at the viewing centre and in that time he's grown to be a fine, healthy young male with a thinnish tawny mane and a long swishing tail. Like most lions he sleeps during the day and hunts at dusk. So far he's only killed zebra and wildebeest. "He's great, isn't he?" said the new assistant. Back home, I glance anxiously in the mirror, poke bits of my body. Still plump and unwrinkled. I'd go for me, if I were a predator. But I'd better contact the field team and start making arrangements.

Jingaling a-Bobbin, Like Apples in a Barrel

Elizabeth phones to ask, will I look after her cats? "I'm awfully busy," I say, thinking she's proposing to arrive on my doorstep, lugging Percy and Lucy in their dual carrier, foisting them on me. "I have to work..."

"I'm going to die," she says. "Probably."

"What! You mean kill yourself?"

"No, Angela. Why would I do that? I can't explain over the phone, but tomorrow may be the last day of my life. And I want to spend it with you, because you're my oldest friend. I thought of Louisa," she adds, "but then I decided no, our relationship is still too young to bear such serious news."

"Well, but I guess if... She'll have to find out some time..."

"So can we meet up?" Elizabeth interrupts me. "I need to book you for the whole of tomorrow. I can't narrow it down any further than that."

Irritated, I sigh. Even before she rang, I had plenty on my mind, now I'm burdened with all these extra doubts and arrangements. But I agree to meet her in a city park tomorrow.

I don't know what Elizabeth's playing at, but she sounded just as normal. She can't really be ill, or she'd surely have told me. She's not usually coy about revealing personal details. Our friendship does indeed go back a long way, to the affair we had at university.

It may be all a pretence, an elaborate ruse, I think. Simply because she wants to meet up with me and I've evaded her the last few times, pleading busy-ness and other engagements. She's exhausting to be with. Tricksy in a childish way. Interrupting small talk, deflating pretension, laughing at the other person, i.e. me. Yet they think well of her at Weymouth University, where she's doing a PhD in web science. Think well of her, with reservations. "Elizabeth, you'll have to get used to our ways of doing things," said one of the lecturers, in response to her suggested radical changes to some university institution. "And we have to get used to you, too. Because we've never met anyone like you before."

Want it or not, my life and Elizabeth's are threads woven together in one garment. She's my friend, that means to some extent I'm her and she's me. Different friends remind us of different parts of ourselves, my friend Jenny once told me – she was training to be a psychotherapist. But then she dropped me, so we no longer hold those kinds of conversation, or any conversations, except in dreams. The Jenny-related part of me has gone wherever it's gone, beyond reminder. Perhaps she too misses the Angela part of herself. But probably she doesn't.

That's why it's so alarming when you introduce two friends with every hope and confidence they'll get along, and instead they dislike each other on sight. As with Jenny and Sue, another friend who's drifted away. Jesus, I've lost so many friends! But not Elizabeth. She refuses to let go of me.

Jenny also claimed the difference between Americans and the English is that Americans have no subtext. ("No subtext! They really don't!") When I phone my American boss to arrange a day's leave, she wishes me a lovely day with my "friend".

Still irritated, I think what if everybody did this? If all my friends current and ex, everybody I've known over the past 56 years, phoned up demanding I spend tomorrow with them, it being their last day – what would I do? How could I possibly divide myself, allot my time so as to satisfy them all, honour what we are/have been to each other?

You're catastrophising, I tell myself. Don't catastrophise! Life is catastrophic enough already. And death is not the end. It certainly isn't. My mother is dead, but just yesterday, waiting in an interminable ticket office queue at Euston, I heard her say brightly inside my head "Number three's providing a stalwart service! He's going great guns!"

We meet outside the park restaurant, below its outdoor seating area. Buffeted by tourist groups, pigeon-pestered. Elizabeth appears relaxed, at ease. The cramped inner-city oasis is her natural environment, or one she's adapted to, just as many types of duck and other ornamental and exotic birds seem at home on the nearby lake. On occasion, shocked tourists have witnessed the pelicans eating pigeons.

The park's flowering cherries are still in pink and white splendour, although plenty of blossom already lies on the grass and the concrete paths. Elizabeth takes my arm and we walk. She has an extra tyre from late-night beer drinking at Weymouth Uni with her mostly male fellow students, and in the lesbian Blush Bar. Black rectangular-framed glasses make her eyes look even smaller and more intense. "I love you," she says.

"I love you, too."

"Of course you do." She laughs. "Don't look so" – pulling a face to show me how ridiculous my expression is. Bridling with pursed mouth, like Maggie Smith in Downton Abbey. Which is absolutely not how I'm feeling.

A robin hops across our path. "That reminds me," Elizabeth says, "I've been composing my Christmas round robin. I know it's a bit early, but..." She sings, a cappella:

> In January I started my semester
> Wearing my sou'wester, in Weymouth by the sea.
> Back to sunny uni, for a web science PhD.
>
> Let's jingaling a-bobbin, like apples in a barrel
> To a Christmas carol, sing ding-a-ding-a-ding
> And a round robin song...

One of these round robins appears in my inbox every year, in the run-up to Christmas. A picture of a robin is attached, plus a music file, Elizabeth accompanying herself on the guitar. When we first met, she told me "I'm going to be a pop star." She also said "I'm gay," which was something nobody ever said in the early 1980s. It caused a strange jolt of feeling to go right through me, exiting between my legs.

She continues singing:

> In March the app designer said hey, you won't last
> many more days,
> Your dying's due in mid May.
> With my isms and ologies, and my data mining
> The Isle of Wight is shining, I'm sailing out to sea.
> Let's jingaling a-bobbin, like apples in a barrel
> To a Christmas carol, sing ding-a-ding-a-ding
> And a round robin song.

Hardly pausing for breath, she demands my opinion. "Is it good?" I know she'll erupt in wounded fury at the slightest hint of criticism.

"It's a work of genius," I tell her.

"Do you think so?"

"I really do."

"Well," she says, pleased, "I've booked some studio

time, so I might record it. If I'm still alive this evening."

"So, the app designer ... why did he tell you such a stupid thing?"

"It's not stupid, it's correct. And he's a she. You might remember I went to South Korea, on a university-funded trip? I presented a research poster at a conference workshop, on how to scale and geolocate incidences of humour in Weibo, the Chinese version of Twitter. This meant standing by my poster for half an hour, waiting for people to ask me questions. Anyway so this woman came along and showed me the app she's been developing. It calculates your life expectancy, not going on statistics but on data readings it takes from your skin and hair. And it's astonishingly accurate!"

"How do you know?"

"She showed me. Her research has been validated. Beyond question, the app works. Unfortunately it gave me only weeks to live. It couldn't say exactly how I'd die – perhaps in an accident, or I'll have a heart attack. Whatever. But soon. It sounds funny, doesn't it? I laughed when she told me. But I believed her."

Elizabeth explains some more about the app, in a blend of technical and mystical language that reminds me of how her singing teacher told her (many years ago) that one must sing from the vagina. Because life passes through it, just as the mouth and throat are the channel through which voice/expression flows. She speaks to you very frankly, I said. Elizabeth replied, she conveyed these things over a period of time.

Now I say, "Oh Elizabeth!"

"Don't worry, don't be sad. I'm not. Are you crying?"

"No, I've got dust in my eye" (true).

We continue walking around the lake. We pause to admire a bed of tulips, red cups of light. We touch the limp young leaves of ashes, limes and sycamores. New holly leaves that don't even have prickles yet. Is life so fragile?

No, it's vigorous and persistent. But wasteful. I'm having problems at work. Errors have been pointed out. Really I should go, it's time. But I always find it hard to leave places.

I'd like to talk my current work predicament over with Elizabeth, but this doesn't seem the right moment. Again I feel faintly annoyed – she's really hogging the spotlight! – and then guilty. I remind myself of all the times she's been there for me, staunchly loyal and supportive. For instance in my twenties when I was chucked out of a lesbian community in Bristol for unsisterly behaviour and didn't know what to do with myself. Elizabeth just walked with me all over the city, not saying anything but keeping at my side. And more recently, when my mother had dementia and while trying to look after her I had a nervous breakdown and thought my face was cracking up, in this very park she told me she couldn't see any lines and that I was beautiful, ageless.

"The cats," she says.

"Of course I'll look after them. If it comes to..." Elizabeth's cats have never been outdoors. Her flat is on the top floor of a converted house. The RSPCA wouldn't let her adopt kittens from them, because of this lack of outdoor space, but the Celia Hammond Trust did – wrongly, in my opinion. Now Percy and Lucy sit on her inside window sills, gaze down at the freshening horse chestnuts, wait for Elizabeth to come home and play with them (or the woman who pops in to feed them when Elizabeth's away), to relieve their boredom. So this is actually a great opportunity for them (and me). How wonderful to see them sniffing grass, pawing earth, lifting their furry faces to the sun!

"Angela." Elizabeth replies to my thoughts. "They're not used to being outside. It would frighten them."

"It might not. Anyway, you can't control what happens after you die."

Elizabeth frowns at this software glitch I've drawn her attention to. "But if they were my children, I could say how I wanted them to be brought up. And you'd have to obey me."

"Only if you'd left instructions to that effect in your will."

"Oh god, my will! I knew I'd forgotten something."

I notice how pale she is. A weird paleness just under the skin, as though a force beyond our universe is siphoning away her blood through invisible holes.

She lies down in a quiet place near the trees and shuts her eyes. "Anyway."

Anyway, that's a very Elizabeth word. She once had a French boyfriend and after they'd been together a few months he asked her "Pourquoi tu dis toujours Hemingway?"

Sitting on the grass beside her, hugging my knees, I wonder, is she even breathing? – and peer at her, trying to detect movement. Then, lying down too, I put my head sideways on her chest – it's quite flat, she has hardly any breasts – listening for a heartbeat, and we just stay like that for a while.

Married to a Carrot

Quite by mistake she'd thrown her wedding ring on the compost heap with some vegetable peelings and it turned up sixteen years later, encircling a fresh young carrot. How wonderful, cried her neighbours and the world's media. From the carrot's point of view, however, things seemed less great. It had considered itself bound in marriage, but now it turned out the woman already had a husband. Also it disliked the flashing cameras, the harsh daylight, the stupid laughter. Depressed, it wilted and withered. Thrown on the compost heap, it lay meditating on love and loss, and making up little poems.

The Moustache Maker's Daughter

Lucy is my name, which means light, and my dad is Ludicrous the moustache maker, so I am Lucy Ludicrous. As a girl, I moulded light into many a useful or pleasing form, dazzling the unwary by making sunbeams zip round corners and scattering sparkles from my fingertips to glitter enticingly on my skin and clothes. Since then I have grown wiser, though I still love a joke. I now intend in all seriousness to describe my life, or at least one day of it – setting the honest truth down here in my occasional book.

The dew is lit by an egg yolk sun just lifted over next-door's chimney, a sun getting ready to fry itself for breakfast with bacon, mushrooms, tomatoes and black pudding, all served on a sky-blue plate. Or anyway, such is my fancy. In a spirit of devilish nonsense, later to be regretted, I conjure up some thistledown baubles and skim them over our neighbour's fence to frizzle his begonias.

I'm on my way to Dad's workshop. As usual I glance up at the house roof, remembering how Mam slipped off it while gathering moss for our Organic Adventures range of moustaches, constructed from natural non-hair materials. Whether her curses (shrieked during that fatal fall) brought bad luck, or the century-end just wasn't the right time to launch such an innovative concept, sadly the new line failed to interest our customers. Mam is buried in the churchyard, a stylised moustache carved over her dates and name, Tootsie Ludicrous. The broken gutter she clutched at desperately still hasn't been mended and in consequence there's now a damp patch on my bedroom ceiling. This is what it's like living with Dad, a man so obsessed by his craft and with profit and loss, he takes no practical steps to weatherproof our dwelling-place.

Having wiped my boots on the tired mat, worn thin from the pressure of many feet (feet that toil here from sunup to sundown and feet of a superior stamp that come to view the moustaches or attend fittings), my first task is to sweep the workshop. Tiny fragments of hair arise from the broom in a prickly cloud and make me sneeze violently while emptying my dustpan into the incinerator.

Next I check that none of the moustaches have been stolen or eaten by rats. Pinned to boards in glass cases like dead insects, they are arranged in six main groups: the Natural, the Hungarian, the Dalí, the English, the Imperial, the Freestyle. Last night after tea Dad plodded off to the workshop and here on the finishing stand is the result of his midnight labours – a fine handlebar, flaunting its bushy exuberance.

Just as I'm blowing on it lightly to add a pleasing lustre, far better than the artificial conditioning imparted by styling mousse or gel, Dad bangs open the door. He grumpily warns me to be careful and not light it up like a gin palace, then falls to working a great pair of 18th century bellows, of crumbly leather and rusty iron. Although unnecessary, since our furnace is connected to the electricity supply, the daily exercise soothes his temper.

Meanwhile and more usefully, for internet orders make up a sizeable part of our business, I fire up the Amstrad; the modem plays its sad violin. A number of today's requests have been discreetly sent in by hair studios, on behalf of third parties – a member of the Indian police force, a couple of high-profile Middle East politicians. I must also keep in regular contact with our suppliers (experienced moustache growers, or outsourcers of growth), dealing with logistics issues and any other problems as they arise. Each supplier is represented by a bobble-headed pin on the map behind my computer. Trondheim has a good sprinkling, also Berlin, Ystad, Anchorage, plus smaller centres of industry such as Thuringia, Zollernalbkreis and Calw. The best coarse moustaches are grown in Siberia, fine-haired ones by Sikh ladies in the West Midlands.

At eleven we take a posset break. Earlier I concocted two healthful possets and these I now pour from a vacuum flask into our moustache-protector mugs, an abandoned sideline. A knock at the door: I startle and Dad spits posset. Enter a gentleman with a high collar and loose fall of necktie, quite the dandy. And come with a view to purchase, for he's young yet, wishful and fretting, only baby down on his upper lip. Yet he has an excellent mouth for a moustache – this I say not snidely but admiring. His face only lacks one hairy ornament to be perfection (I discount beards, which although they complement our craft are repulsive to me personally). Elsewise he's the excelsior.

"What do you want?" Dad barks at our prospective customer.

He speaks out bold: "A moustache."

"Well you've come to the right place," I say with loud cheerfulness, to drown out Dad.

"Thank you. I hope so." His eye lights on the finishing stand and my parent's new creation. Awed, he ventures near and asks permission to touch. Dad shrugs – his most fulsome gesture of civility.

Our Adonis is enraptured by the handlebar and only unwillingly dissuaded from its purchase. His face is unsuited to this item, I tell him bluntly. Its ideal wearer is a carnival strongman or medal-decorated veteran, or failing one of those a grizzled père de famille. He then ponders a Pancho Villa, foolishly fingers a Fu Manchu. But guided by me, he at last opts for a classic Chevron: suave yet possessed of gravitas, exactly the right follicular architecture for a baby face. And as twas ever truly said, the moustache maketh the man.

Dad triples the recommended retail price, adds a double service charge (accounting for us both) and VAT (which we're not registered for) plus a large 'courtesy gratuity'. Presenting our card reader, I bashfully avert my gaze while the Chevron inserts his Mastercard and taps in the code. Et voilà! I fold the receipt of our transaction into his palm. We send him off happy, with a clanking carrier bagful of salves and potions.

"Well, Dad" I say jokingly, "your new handlebar is king of our collection."

A smile creeps to one corner of Dad's mouth and nestles there, like a dormouse in winter, as he shakes his head. Undeniably the handlebar is a mo with mojo, but: "I've known better," he says. "Ah. Once I made a moustache to go courting in. Got a hedge wizard to put a glamour on it. Sunlight broke through rain at the moment he cast the spell and it took strong. The moustache leapt to my lip and fixed itself. Down the road I saw a pretty lass and tipped her a wink. Your mam."

His tale makes me guffaw, yet prompts sad reflection on how time destroys our appearances. For that saucy young coxcomb is now a wreck of a man. "What happened to the moustache, Dad?" I ask.

"Duty done, it scarpered. Never laid eyes on it since." Off he goes to the alehouse, to make our profits behave likewise. I sigh, put all in order and lock up, cogitating the while on that tricksy moustache. For sure it pulled the wool over Mam's eyes – a saying that also concerns false hair, as it derives from the ancient practice of tilting an opponent's wig.

But to think of my grumbly old dad playing Prince Charming! A-chortle at this idea, I go in search of the garments he wore in his jaunty youth. I guess they'll still be in his clothes chest, and sure enough. In a twinkling I exchange womanish for mannish apparel. Peering in the mould-spotted glass, I nod at myself. S/he only lacks one vital accessory, I think, but then my nostrils twitch, prompting me to look again. I've gained – and my reflection has too – a moustache! What type of moustache? Hard to say, for it keeps subtly changing, as though to avoid definition. If pressed I'd have to term it the Elusive.

Well! All kitted out and male-beautified, it'd be a shame to hide indoors. So I saunter into the centre, which takes nine minutes. Chainstored much like everywhere else, our town's only novelty feature is its rustic benches. These are fixed with their backs to the road, annoying the old folk, who would rather sit watching the traffic than be knee-bumped by passing shoppers. However, today one of these shunned benches hosts a courting couple: blonde Susie and the Chevron. As I draw closer, Susie spots me too and her pansy eyes open eloquently wide. You wait years for an attractive man to enter the vicinity and then along come two at once! Unlike our local bus service, which is on the whole regular and reliable.

The Chevron struggles under a disadvantage – his moustache is falling off. (Cheap glue's to blame for its slippage: I silently curse my absent parent.) Holding it in place with one finger, he strives to appear at perfect ease. Susie's glance wavers between us, she seems inclined to favour yours truly. I stare hard in the butcher's shop window – pale chitterlings and even paler tripe, faggots in their white webs – then duck into the baker's.

Behind the display counter is Nush, my old school pal, stout of figure and pretty of face. I pull at my moustache, studying her pastries, pies and patties, her tartlets, quiches and mini-pizzas. Muffins and turnovers, calzone and kugelhopf, Parmesan biscuits and spinachy spanakopita. Chocolate brownies and gingerbread houses, pink eclairs and lemon cupcakes. Her strawberry meringue kisses, her marmalade tray bake.

"Anything take your fancy?"

"I'm still deciding."

"Today's specials..." she begins. Laughter chokes information. Of course she knows me. We sat at the same double desk in the pre-fab classroom and I stuck paper moustaches on my face to amuse her. She cracked up when they fell off.

"A selection?"

"Please."

She pops in an extra cheddar scroll and spins the bag around, twisting its corners. Meanwhile I search the pockets of young-Dad's costume, hoping to light upon a florin or doubloon. But no, empty.

"Um."

"I wouldn't think of charging you. Have a nice day."

I stumble away quite dizzy, whether from the oven's heat or the touch of her fingers. Before exiting, I turn and wink. The moustache twirls as male magic muscles in; Nush gasps and claps a hand under her breast. Too late, the caged bird's flown.

Susie's been watching the door, so as I emerge I'm caught between a rock and a soft place (which of these endures?). But I fail inspection; the blonde huffs in disappointment. I'm sans moustache, is the reason: duty done, it's vanished. Synchronically and right opposite, Dad lurches through the swing doors of the Cock and Anchor. Fearful of him seeing me and consequent tedious explanation, or a medical disaster, I dip and dive, scoot and skedaddle (ancient meaning, to avoid Dad).

Eventide. Restored to womanish dishevelment, I'm sitting in our garden. Nature's fade bestows quiet though unprayerful reflection. I watch the fat sun crossly squeeze between two 'detached' houses on the new estate. Remembering that long-ago time when Mam and I, perched in the sand dunes, saw it melt gleaming gold into the sea. Mam then arose and shook her skirts. "That's it," she said, ever practical, dismissing melancholy. And the wind blew chill as we stumbled back to our B&B.

I hear a pattering – rain? Small things falling all around, impact of the compact. One strikes my nose, tumbles into my lap. A slug. Neighbour's tossing them over, not in compliment but as revenge missiles. Cautiously I creep to the fence, put my eye to a punched-out knothole. His back door slams. I observe florals all singed and sickly, begonias begone.

Shame on you, Lucy – more rightly to be called Lucifer! That poor man hid his heart among red and white blossoms, therein located the Lovely. And you have pulverised them!

Humbly repentant and mentally scheduling a visit to the garden centre, I pick up the slugs (using my light-generating powers to find where they've fallen) bucket them and set out for the park. I cut down Mudd Lane to Fourways, where a lamppost now stands in place of the old gallows. And leaning against that lamppost is the Chevron.

I bid him good evening, he answers politely, we converse and he soon tells me the reason he's hanging around (ha ha). Since the town has no decent eateries, Susie arranged to meet him later and went home for her tea. We chat jollily, our eyes exchanging romantic suggestions. I perceive that I might have him. Unluckily at this point I make a crude joke about penises, tipping the bucket to reveal its wriggly contents. He turns faint and slides down the lamppost. Ah well.

His moustache is awry. Which reminds me, earlier I purloined a bottle of our best glue from Dad's secret stash. I tuck this into his pocket and leave him to Susie.

Lucy Ludicrous, I sigh, your love of jesting will be your ruination. But then I think of Nush and her cinnamon and raisin swirl cake, whereupon I grin and go on my way, bucket swinging. Tis fine to be merry-alive and running an independent business, in the early 21st century.

A Mild Critique of the Parole System

I have applied for parole again, though of course I won't get it. But they like you to try, because it means filling out forms and kowtowing to the board. I've examined the relevant leaflet and booklet. "Mere eligibility for parole will not entitle a prisoner to parole." That's said three times, in varying language apart from the word parole. So basically, these handouts convey you'd be foolish to get your hopes up. But I never did before and won't this time either, since I know that good prisoner though I am, my one quiet murder is remembered in the world outside our yellow brick haven.

She heard every word I thought. It grew unbearable, living close to someone so perspicacious. If you want to kill me, she said, do it now before the News. Her mind was going, in the way old people's minds do, but even in that altered condition she was highly intelligent. I could wonder forever at her knowledge.

If I'd known some techniques perhaps I'd have done it more delicately, but as it was she didn't suffer much. I remember standing at the bay window in our lounge – by then I thought of it as ours – and seeing the police about to ring our doorbell; they'd left the gate open. I'd just got the front garden looking nice, using those plants that go on year after year, repeating themselves dutifully. Perennials, that's what they're called. If nobody's dug them up yet, they'll still be there.

Broken Thing

As one long prepared, and graced with courage,
say goodbye to her, the Alexandria that is leaving.
— The God Abandons Anthony, by C.P. Cavafy

She had a pot she liked. Copied from an ancient pot, which had lain broken for centuries, perhaps damaged for much longer than whole, and never truly restored to itself. People in ancient Alexandria had touched and held the original unbroken pot, and kept something in it. But they weren't us. Our pot wasn't that pot.

She cradled our pot in her hands like a priestess and said we must never break this cup (she called the pot a cup). It would be such bad luck, she said. I slouched in my chair, overpowered by the marshy stink of Nile coming off her arms and neck. We'd bought this perfume and the pot on the same terrifyingly expensive visit to the British Museum's gift shop. They had tester bottles. One scent had been found in a salesman's case on the Titanic, another exhumed from a pyramid.

Ayesha was my first long-term girlfriend, I didn't have much experience. But I knew enough to handle the pot carefully. A few weeks later I saw it lying in pieces on the table.

"Did you break it?" I asked her.

She just looked at me. Tense and sharp-edged.

"The pot? I mean cup?" Silence.

Next day the pot was whole again, though with visible cracks.

"So you glued it back together?" She didn't reply.

Ground had changed to swamp. Terrible atmosphere. I know now that this is fairly normal in relationships, and usually things turn out OK if you just wait, keep calm, don't let fear dictate your actions, but back then I panicked easily. It felt impossible to stay inside the house. I couldn't breathe. So I went for a walk.

The only walk in our cramped neighbourhood of small terraced houses was over a main road, past a playground and some littered grass, then along by the river. High tide concealed all the rusty skeletons of things in the mud, so for a while you might forget their existence. They were still there, though.

My gut spasmed. How come I was so much at her mercy? Because she was better at covering stuff up, not revealing her own fears and uncertainties, if she had any, and this made her seem very strong. Women didn't understand how strong they were. They could reject you and make you feel like shit... Eventually the path ended and the river went on alone. A couple of benches marked this final giving-up place.

Although when I go down I can't stop myself, I try to be reasonable. I sat on one of the benches and examined my assumptions. Was she angry with me? Yes. Justifiably? Not unless I'd been insensitive. Had I? No, I didn't think so – because in fact I was ultra-sensitive to her and her moods. The tide must be on the turn, all the boats were pointing sideways. Moved by a larger force and yet not drifting freely. Tethered to their fate.

Then I thought, is it even true she broke the pot? Maybe it just fell apart. In which case, she'll have assumed I'm the guilty one and be waiting for me to apologise. All a stupid misunderstanding, easily resolved. The river glittered, the boats swung around.

Ayesha was frowning at the mirror in our hallway. As she turned to me, her face smoothed into blankness. Although I didn't know quite what that look of hers meant, in a way it was self-explanatory. Like a corpse in the mud.

"About the pot," I said, "I mean the cup."

"It really doesn't matter, Den." She went to the kitchen.

I followed her, propelled by some crazy determination. "You think I broke the cup."

"No I don't."

"Then why are you upset?"

"It's not even worth discussing. Anyway I'm not upset. In the least." She ran a glass of water from the tap and drank from it "How's your website?"

"I've been…"

"Good." She pushed past me. In the corridor she turned. "Stop thinking, Den. If you think about things too much, they might come true."

What did she mean?

That same evening I went for a drink with Chris, a good mate. The Watery Moon had recently been refurbished and live music acts introduced. Personally I'd preferred the old gloomy interior, its stained carpet and acts of violence, such as glassing – many was the night I'd spent in A&E with Chris, after one of his seemingly innocuous remarks had provoked a drinker by the bar – even the occasional murder. But that evening Chris took his pint to where jazz was being played in the former darts area. So I ended up talking to Jonah, a friend of his from work.

Jonah had small eyes and soft feminine skin. He was smoking roll-ups and drinking a type of beer made by Trappist monks. We talked deeply. He agreed that since things were innately unstable and impermanent they could often break by themselves, without human agency.

"I've known glasses shatter when they were just standing on a table. And windows crack. Mind you, with my mum … there was always a lot of tension."

"Yeah?"

"Yeah. So what'll you do now? Move out?"

"No! It's just that..." But the more I tried to explain, the more Jonah persisted in his obtuseness. "Yeah, women, they always want you to talk about things. Talk and talk. It's a form of madness." He sipped his Trappist ale. I decided he wasn't such a great fount of spiritual wisdom after all.

"Thinking about your pot," he resumed. I felt hopeful again. "Have you got a cat?"

"No."

"Right. Just a thought. Cats often knock things off shelves."

News reached us in fragments and murmurs. Lost, disappeared. One of the jazz instruments, the double bass. Taken? The player had left it for five minutes, gone to the bar and on his return... Police called, search instigated. Chris joined us: "I knew something like this would happen." He thought the pub was built on a vortex, or a crack in time and space. Below our conscious radar, malicious spirits dance. The theft merely a symptom... ramblings fairly typical of both Chris and pub conversations.

How could a double bass just vanish? Nobody had seen it go. The player looked as if his legs had walked off by themselves. Someone announced "We're going to search the streets." No point, I thought. And yet, what did I know? The double bass might be lurking in some alley or cul de sac, poking from a wheelie bin. It might have formed a new constellation in the night sky. For all I knew.

A bloke continued loudly and sorrowfully telling the story of his marriage break-up. "While I was asleep, they were fucking..." How traumatic, I thought. But at least she didn't just withdraw from him and go quiet.

When we first got together, love energy flowed between us like music. I didn't mind Ayesha's untidiness. I loved how she walked around our bedroom naked, with the curtains open, not caring about the opposite houses. She connected me with the world, with life. Encouraged me to go self-employed, paid the rent and the bills. Sometimes after she'd left for work I would hear tinkling laughter like elves in an enchanted forest. Downstairs if I was upstairs, or vice versa. I hadn't heard it recently, though.

Back home, I found the stairs too hard to climb and fell on the sofa. It caught and held me in a light grasp, but with all the strength of its hidden springs, its coffee-stained fabric. Destined to move on its little wheels, yet content to stay still. Unlike the lounge, which kept coming and going in sick transit. From this whirligig, something emerged – the pot, high up next to some books.

Warily, I approached the bookcase and took it down. Reverently I held it in both hands. Warm love flowed into me and I belched. The pot was decorated with Egyptian scenes: a river at low tide, a marshy landscape. A heron like one I often saw standing hunched and motionless, watching a rivulet in the mud. For a moment, I had the feeling I could disappear into that ancient yet so familiar world…

And then I dropped it. Smash on the tiled hearth.

No doubt or confusion this time. I'd broken the pot. Me.

Destroyed beyond any chance of repair. Shards and slivers.

In my dreams that night, curled foetally on the sofa, the pot kept breaking and then becoming mysteriously whole, only to break again. Woken by a gasp, I heard Ayesha sweeping up the fragments with dustpan and brush. I kept my eyes closed against morning reality.

Over the following days we had some conversations. Not about the pot, though. She didn't mention the pot at all. Not even to tell me I was an idiot, laughingly or in anger. So we were talking but not talking. I felt more hopeful when we were apart. Then I could dwell on memories of nakedness and elfin laughter. Or further back – her serious gaze at the computer screen in those days when she had no idea I was watching her, or that I existed.

At the British Museum ("We never do anything cultural, Den. The whole of London's on our doorstep, we're missing all these opportunities. Well I'll go by myself if you won't come. No get off me. I'm serious…") we'd seen an exhibition. They'd found a sphinx, other statues and some ancient buildings all hidden in murky water near the harbour in Alexandria, where Cleopatra was Queen. The Sphinx has the haunches of a lion, the wings of a great bird and the face of a woman. She poses difficult riddles. If you can't answer them, she eats you.

I went for a walk and slumped on a bench near the playground. A badly placed bench, since a concrete wall now obscured most of the river from view. Maybe they put the bench here before they built the wall. The wall itself was quite boring to look at.

A woman came and sat down next to me, her hands thrust into her coat pockets. I caught a whiff of Nile before I saw who it was. The smell of loss.

She let the sun fall on her face. "It's really quite nice out here." She took a breath.

"You're leaving, aren't you?" I said, before she could say it, and she faintly smiled. Then I understood for the first time that I – or more accurately it, the situation including me – just wasn't right for her. The rented house and the clumsy beta male. We'd somehow quenched her. She used to be so alive.

I thought I might as well apologise. "I'm sorry I broke the pot."

"Never mind, that really doesn't matter." She kissed my cheek. "You'll work it out."

After she'd gone, I stood and leaned against the wall,

my arms on a rail. How fast and far beyond me she'd already moved. And yet her future was clearer to me than my own. Easy to predict, for instance, that she'd marry someone else. I thought for her wedding present I'd get her another pot from the British Museum. Or go diving near the harbour of Alexandria, to retrieve some similar priceless thing from an underwater palace. That would be a romantic gesture.

Then I noticed a large object afloat in the middle of the river, being carried along fast. It was the double bass.

From a distance it seemed whole and undamaged, although obviously not in its ideal environment. Remembering its owner's stricken bereaved face I knew I should do something, but instead I gazed listlessly after the vanishing instrument.

One day, I thought, I'll ask her to explain what happened between us. When I'm ready to. Of course her version of events is probably quite different from mine. Anyone who's ever been with anyone knows you remember things differently from how the other person remembers them, or you remember different things.

Babylon

This is nothing against Bernard, my brother who we're both very fond of. He acted from the best of motives throughout, I'm sure. First he bought us a teapot, a green one. Just as an ornament, it was fine. But he insisted on us using it. He was over from New York for a couple of weeks, on a business trip, but staying in our semi-detached house in North Acton. I sensed my sister-in-law's influence. And sure enough.

Rose says it's unsociable not to use a teapot, Bernard said. The problem here was, though, my husband Joe likes his tea very weak. Just show it the teabag. The thought of tea stewing in a pot gives him the willies. So he pretended he didn't really like tea and he'd have Nescafé instead. Then Bernard said, I'm afraid I'm a bit of a snob about coffee. Meaning, Rose is a snob about coffee. He bought us a grinder, a filter machine and some Guatemalan coffee beans. We sipped politely, trying not to wince.

Laura phoned: Mum, you've got to stand up to him. You know Dad won't. I re-entered the sitting room to find Bernard criticising our flowery wallpaper, our curtains and our carpets. You're only in your forties, not your eighties.

Well, I admit we haven't changed much since we moved in. The former owner died, so we inherited a lot of her stuff. But I like the sense of continuity. Patterned carpets are coming back into fashion, I told Bernard. It was true, I'd read it in a colour supplement. Not these ones, he said.

Joe's parents rang, their usual weekly phone call. His mum is very nice. His dad harrumphs in the background. They used to live in Africa and Joe's father remembered a tribal saying, "Feast your guest as a prince for two days and on the third morning, hand him the hoe." I laughed – but thinking of my plants, I thought no. As it turned out, that was prescient of me.

Then Bernard shipped us off to a country house hotel. How generous of him, we thought, to show his appreciation. Only we both felt it was a bit peculiar, him staying in our house while we're in a hotel. But only those dates were available. A sense of dread prevented me from fully enjoying the swimming pool, the health club and the extensive grounds. When we got back, the first thing I noticed was skips outside the house and the second thing – which struck Joe first – the house itself had been painted turquoise (over the pebbledash), with gold window sills and frames, and gold barge boards behind gold guttering. It looked dreadful.

A surprise makeover. The TV designer people like to have a theme and in our case it was Babylon. The back garden was covered in glittery plastic decking. Our old shed had gone, replaced by a gold temple. Inside, the stripped floorboards looked cold. The sitting room was where they'd really gone to town, with a mural of Babylon – more temples – and hanging baskets everywhere. It struck me at once these were impractical, because of the watering. But nobody had thought of that.

Faced by the TV cameras, of course we said how wonderful it all was. Modern and yet linked with an ancient civilisation. The old place was due for a change! Joe said, and we all laughed.

We waved from the door, then went back inside. No sofa, only an uncomfortable metal thing. By the mural of Babylon we sat down and cried, remembering our lovely house.

In Bed with Miss Lucas

Charlotte was in the apple garth, removing a comb from one of the beehives, when she noticed something moving in a shady place beneath the trees. A shape that separated, becoming two, then merged again. A thing composed of humanity, of partly naked flesh. It was Mr Collins and her brother William.

Her arms were sleeved in crawling bees – she wore no protection, only a muslin smock over her dress – and intent not to disturb them more than the task required, she remained still. Honey dripped from the comb.

Mr Collins shouted out, then uttered a blasphemy, while slapping at his nether parts. A bee had stung him. They are intelligent, even witty creatures; this one died for its joke.

"Don't tell, Charlotte, because I never tell on you." She did not at once understand William's passing remark, made under his breath. When the meaning of his words became clear to her, she was outraged by the sordid comparison.

"It is an entirely different thing!" she muttered to herself in the laundry room, while attending to her brother's seducer. A blue bag had been found effective to draw the sting and soothe the hurt. Now Mr Collins was lecturing her upon her good fortune; upon the affability and condescension of Lady Catherine de Bourgh. Would the man never be quiet?

She returned the bottle of saltpetre to the shelf; he proposed to her. It was not romantic. This was Lady Catherine's own suggestion, apparently; made upon receiving the news of Miss Elizabeth Bennet's refusal of her protégé. He proudly displayed Lady Catherine's letter, of which she could make out very little, since – as was her Ladyship's habit – it was narrowly crossed and untidily written. However, she was not insensible to the many advantages of such an arrangement; principally, the freedom it would give her. She took a moment to consider, then accepted his proposal – or rather, his patron's decision.

Lady Catherine had already written several letters to Charlotte, containing detailed instructions on such matters as the keeping of poultry and self-education. Miss Lucas had not perused these with any great attention: better to preserve the flattering idea of this great lady's favour than to consider seriously whether the relationship would be likely to promote long-lasting happiness and content.

As for Mr Collins: well. Her parents would be delighted, since he would succeed to the possession of Longbourn after Mr Bennet's death, and the match would thereby allow them to triumph over their neighbours. The younger girls might now form hopes of *coming out* a year or two sooner than they might otherwise have done; and the boys would be relieved from their apprehension of Charlotte's dying an old maid. The least agreeable circumstance in the business was the surprise it must occasion to Elizabeth Bennet, whose friendship she valued beyond that of any other person, by whose opinions she was most often guided, and whose trust she had betrayed.

Elizabeth set down the candle. She said, "Lydia will keep poor Jane up half the night, I daresay, with her usual nonsensical chatter of officers and gentlemen."

"It was good of Jane, to allow me to usurp her place in your bed."

"Jane is always good," Elizabeth sighed. "Too good, I sometimes think."

Charlotte unlaced her friend's corset, kissed the back of her neck, and left her standing in her chemise. "I must speak to you, Eliza, of a matter which perhaps will shock you." She then disclosed the matter of her own recent correspondence with Lady Catherine.

Elizabeth had often felt that Miss Lucas's nature was very different from her own; but that she could encourage such a person, seemed almost as far from possibility as that Elizabeth could encourage Lady Catherine herself, and her astonishment was consequently so great as to overcome at first the bounds of decorum, and she could not help crying out,

"Lady Catherine de Bourgh! my dear Charlotte – impossible!"

Miss Lucas seemed a little perturbed on receiving so direct a reproach; though, as it was no more than she expected, she soon regained her composure, and crossed an ankle over her knee before replying,

"Why should you be surprised, my dear Eliza? Do you consider yourself to be the only person with a claim to my attentions? Or do you think it incredible that Lady Catherine should be able to procure any woman's good opinion, because she has not been so happy as to secure yours?"

But Elizabeth had now recollected herself, and making a strong effort, was able to assure Miss Lucas with tolerable firmness that the prospect of their intimacy was highly grateful to her, and that she wished her all imaginable happiness.

"Thank you."

"Be so good as to tell me, Charlotte, how the two of you became acquainted?"

"Lady Catherine heard of me by reputation," Charlotte replied delicately. "We have exchanged portraits. You may recall that Maria sketched me in the character of Rosalind? She prefers that one above the rest."

"She will make you cut off your hair." Elizabeth got into bed and punched one of the pillows.

"I should not mind it." Miss Lucas joined her friend.

"You must know that she is a relation of Mr Darcy."

"Yes, and I intend you to marry him, so that we may continue to meet often."

"I am afraid, then, Charlotte, you will be sadly disappointed."

The conversation broke off and did not resume for a while, partly because Miss Lucas had her hand over Elizabeth's mouth, to stop her from screaming out loud. At length she said, "Well?"

Attempting to control her breath, Elizabeth said, "I will think on the matter, Charlotte."

"Good. I have not yet talked to you of Mr Collins."

"Pray do not talk of him at all."

"I must; and then we will leave the subject entirely."

Jane confessed herself a little surprised at the prospect of a liaison between Miss Lucas and Lady Catherine; but she said less of her astonishment than of her earnest desire for their happiness; nor could Elizabeth persuade her to consider it as unlikely.

"My dear Jane! Your sweetness and disinterestedness are really angelic. But in truth, it is impossible for any one woman to retain Miss Lucas's undivided affections. She is not romantic."

"Oh, my poor Lizzie."

"I am now tempted to make another acquaintance myself. What think you of Miss Bingley?"

"Well..." Jane hesitated.

"Of course I am joking."

❦

Lady Catherine had expressed an inclination to see Pemberley again, and was determined that Charlotte should accompany her.

"The family is not down for the summer, or certainly I should not think of it. Miss Elizabeth Bennet, as she was before she ensnared my nephew into this disgraceful marriage, must not expect to be noticed by his family and friends, having willfully acted against the inclinations of all. Nay, she must be censured, slighted and despised by everyone connected with him."

Charlotte said nothing in return – her mind was too full for conversation, her spirits too low – and both remained silent as they entered the park. A stream of some natural importance was swelled into greater, but without any artificial appearance. Its banks were neither formal, nor falsely adorned. How unlike Rosings Park, Lady Catherine's residence!

As their carriage drew near to the house, Charlotte was overcome by apprehension lest they should have been misinformed. She longed to see Elizabeth again, yet dreaded the thought of meeting her in company with Mr Darcy, or in Lady Catherine's presence. That Mr Darcy was equally anxious to prevent such a gathering, she felt sure.

Once admitted into the hall, they were greeted by the housekeeper. As they passed into other rooms, Charlotte observed less of splendour, but more real elegance, than she was accustomed to see at Rosings. Her own home on Lady Catherine's estate was rather small, but well built and convenient, and when Mr Collins could be forgotten – as he often was – it provided great comfort.

Lady Catherine lamented some changes made to the disposition of the furniture in her nephew's house, and deplored the old-fashioned curtains, while attributing all perceived lapses in taste to Elizabeth. "She has improved the place so little and wrought such harm!" Unable to listen further, Charlotte excused herself and hurried from the room. She saw the housekeeper's surprise, and Lady Catherine looked very displeased. Quickly, she left the house and walked away, hardly knowing which direction she took.

A circuit walk led to a path that descended among hanging woods. She crossed the river by a simple bridge, and followed a narrow walk. Upon entering a clearing, to her great surprise, there before her she saw Elizabeth and another woman. They were within ten yards of her, and so abrupt was her arrival that it was impossible to avoid an encounter. Charlotte's eyes met Elizabeth's, and the cheeks of each were overspread with the deepest blush. For a moment, both seemed immoveable from surprise, but shortly recovering themselves, they advanced and spoke, if not in terms of perfect composure, at least of perfect civility.

Mrs Darcy was very obviously expecting a child, but said nothing of her condition. She introduced Charlotte to her companion, Mr Darcy's sister Georgiana. The young woman was also blushing, though for no apparent reason. Her manners were unassuming and gentle, and she seemed exceedingly shy. She curtseyed and held out her hand; Charlotte, without thinking, took and kissed it. This made Georgiana gasp, and Elizabeth smile.

In the years that immediately followed, Charlotte received several letters from Elizabeth, giving information about her growing family; and these never failed to mention Georgiana. "My sister asks to be remembered to you – commands me to say that – would be glad to have news of you." Charlotte kept the letters in her desk. She perceived that Mrs Darcy was hard put to it to dampen the enthusiastic admiration of her young relative for a person she had met just once in a glade.

Charlotte herself had thought Miss Darcy pleasant enough, with sense and good humour in her face: but she wished only for the friend of her own youth. Too well persuaded of the value of all she had lost, or willfully thrown away, she mourned her own perverseness of feeling, while knowing how improbable it was that they should ever again be united on terms of mutual cordiality.

Their correspondence ceased for a while; until at last Mrs Darcy wrote again. This time, there was no message from Georgiana. She had moved, with a friend, to Llangollen in Wales, and was living there in sweet retirement – according to Elizabeth, "in neatness, elegance and taste".

Upon the sudden death of Mr Collins – from a cold he caught while reciting the burial service, together with many encomiums, at Lady Catherine's graveside, in a sharp easterly wind – Mr Darcy travelled to Rosings from Derbyshire. He brought his private chaplain to chant Mr Collins's own requiem, and his wife to console the grieving widow as best she might.

The years had wrought their changes and Mr Darcy, now florid and portly, went off to the funeral in the highest good humour, without betraying any apprehension as to the wisdom or the propriety of leaving Elizabeth alone with Mrs Collins. Alone they effectively were in the drawing room of Rosings, for Lady Catherine's daughter Anne, grown from a peevish and sickly young woman to an autocratic matron, was employing her time usefully in itemising the linen cupboard.

After a little silence, Charlotte said, "You are as beautiful as ever, Eliza."

"My dear, you flatter me. When a woman has three grown-up daughters, she ought to give over thinking of her own beauty."

"I don't believe you ever thought of it much."

Elizabeth picked at the chair's arm. "Lady Catherine's death must have dealt you a great blow."

"It was a surprise. One evening we quarrelled over a trifle, as was not unusual. I went up to bed, taking leave of her with very little courtesy, and she died of a stroke, in that chair." Elizabeth stood up quickly. "We found her in the morning, still seated upright, as though turned to stone."

"How horrible!"

"Let us talk of more cheerful matters. Have you heard lately from Miss Darcy?"

"Yes, I thank you. She is well, and I believe most happy. What a charming view from this window! And what will you do now, Charlotte? How will you live?"

"Both my husband and Lady Catherine have left me well provided for. Perhaps I shall take lodgings in Bath."

"Will you live alone?"

"I think so. Unless you will come with me."

Elizabeth did not turn around. "There was a time – we could perhaps – but it is too late now."

"I did not know such a thing was possible."

"Sometimes one must force a way to others' acceptance. I never loved my husband so well as when he gave way at last to Georgiana's pleas. Otherwise I think she must have died of grief, for she would not part with her friend. Ah – it is a pity, a pity." Elizabeth walked up the room and down again. "I wish that custom did not forbid us to attend Mr Collins's funeral, for at least then we might get some fresh air. To be confined indoors – unbearable!"

"Shall we go upstairs? It is lighter there."

"Oh! Very well."

As they ascended the grand staircase, Charlotte said, "I could not love her."

"Of course not. It was never in your nature to suffer another's will to override your own. But the question remains, Charlotte, whether you are capable of giving your heart to anyone."

"Did you give yours – I mean, to your husband?"

"Yes. We were very much in love. I did not marry him at your bidding."

"I never believed so."

"And yet; and yet. This is hard to say. Well. My thoughts oftentimes flew away to you. I remembered how after we had – been together, in bed – you would wait, and after a little while, you would ask, 'Are you ready for me again?' And that helped; if you take my meaning. It raised up my nature."

They crossed the upper landing and entered a large, airy bedchamber. Charlotte locked the door behind them. She said, "You need not be afraid. Catherine never came in here."

"What is that to me?" Elizabeth held out her hand for the key.

Charlotte gave it to her. "And you likewise would never suffer another's will to override yours."

Elizabeth held the key against her lips for a few moments, considering; then she walked to the window and placed it on the sill. She threw open the casement. At once the fresh and sweet smell of lilac rushed into the room, with the singing of many birds.

"Are you ready for me again?" Charlotte asked her.

The Society of Lost Souls

The advertisement had popped up in her Facebook news feed – Society of Lost Souls. And here it was. It actually did exist. A discreet entrance on a busy road, the name etched on a tarnished brass rectangle fixed to a plain door.

Pressing the bell she heard a distant chime. The door clicked open and she entered a vast hall. Sunlight pouring down from a cupola failed to obliterate the many shadows – young and old, men and women. They scattered at her approach, pulling down their sleeves to hide their wrists or turning up their collars.

The Society Rulebook opened in front of her like a flower. It hung in the air, faintly vibrating as though borne by invisible hummingbirds. Pages turned rapidly, stopping at Rules for Rescuers in large type, centred. They were: Eat Nothing. Touch Nobody. Don't Look Round. The book flapped shut and withdrew.

Plates laden with bright, sweet things – peppermint creams, lollies, candy necklaces, fairy cakes – came floating past temptingly. Except she wasn't tempted. Whoever ran the Society of Lost Souls obviously thought she was still a child, or childish. Knowing this emboldened her like a disguise.

As the rejected plates all huffily flew away she noticed a woman in a flowery dress beckoning to her. An old woman – no a young one, gentle and sad. Have you seen my sister, the girl asked. Do you know where she is? The woman cooed like a woodpigeon: through the door, through the door. She moved aside and there it was, a door set neatly in a panelled wall. Its round bronze handle almost froze the girl's hand. She went through and fell into darkness. Then she forgot most things except why she was here and who for. Everything became nothing.

She woke in another in-between place, a corridor, and hoped she hadn't done anything wrong. Voices chattered like sparrows in a nearby room; she peered through the doorway. There was Lucy in a blue beaded dress, 1920s style. Smiling, about to read one of her poems aloud. A library or clubroom, it seemed to be. Dinner-jacketed men lounged in armchairs.

Lucy! Lucy! – she tried to call. No sound came, she was voiceless here, but Lucy turned. Pages slipped out of her hands and fluttered down, vanishing before they touched the inlaid parquet floor.

She repeated her sister's name and Lucy drifted towards her. Follow me, she said, and resolutely led the way. But then, ah, her heart wavered. She looked behind, glanced back down the corridor. Farewell it must now be. Her sister blew her a kiss and ran off laughing.

A Bit of Tragedy

Our jagged bay has a nibbled look, so we're called Bite. It's a little out-of-the-way seaside place, you won't have heard of. With fine grey mousy sand. There used to be something magical about this grey sand, but now there isn't. It's got dirty over the past couple of decades and I've lost the glamour of childish perceptions. Unlike those fortunate ones who've never been wronged or abandoned.

Up and down our beach my sister Lucie would walk. Gazing wistfully out to sea, as though hoping to glimpse the mast of a ship, longing ever for the return of her sailor lover. She had no lover, I might add, nor did she want one. She was quite independent and self-reliant. She walked for six hours a day if the weather was fine, otherwise two hours, wearing a long white cotton skirt with a deep flounce and a white corset top that emphasised her breasts. Which, of course, as her brother I shouldn't even have been noticing.

I don't want to work in a shop, she'd told me. I knew this already, because she'd been sacked from the Seahorse gift and card emporium for having neglected her duties at till and counter, her gaze ever straying to the wide ocean.

On sunny days, she carried a straw hat with a blue ribbon, or when it was a bit chilly she might wrap herself in a white shawl crocheted by our mother, years before. And the sea poured in, transparent green or dark as rage and jealousy as the case might be.

When the gulls laugh, Bite isn't a place for tragedy. The air bright, the windows crystalled with salt. We live just past the church, up a narrow street. Once I slept under the eaves, close to the stars it felt, although our dwelling crouches in the terrace like a small bullied creature. Then I moved downstairs to Lucie's old room. She occupies Ma's chamber, when she's not on the beach, or gone. That first night I missed her light sniffle-snuffle beyond the parting wall, it took me ages to drift off.

Next morning, after I'd riddled the ashes, I sat and gnawed my fist. Bite has any town's usual complement of murdered females. Jen Wool the clarinet player, strangled and her corpse left underneath the bandstand. Anna Mistle who took a shortcut down Anchor Alley after pub closing time. Clarissa Bunter going door to door for a charity sky-dive, invited in by somebody. All so pretty, brave and fragile. Others too, in the past year. Had Lucie joined their sad company, her ghost flying in the air like spume blown off the waves?

I'd left a batch of dragons in the kiln overnight, but they'd cracked and were lying in pieces. Salt moisture had got into the clay, or I just hadn't prepared it well. Either way, I was to blame. Loser, loser, a voice in my head mocked me. A sufferer of losses, that's me. Damaged, bereft. And now... Trying to shake off my apprehension, I went along the beach. The sea was all a-dance. Lucie loved rough weather and adventures. Maybe she'd got cut off by the tide while exploring a cove. Or a reaching wave had gathered her to the sea's broody breast.

A whelk-abandoned shell held to my ear. A murmur, a memory. Lucie sighing: "This job's OK except that he spies on me. He lurks in the dunes. I wish he wouldn't."

Have you seen that picture of grains of sand magnified? Branching trees, whirling stars and oh such colours! My sister bestowed like hidden glory upon our dull strand. At least I felt it was so.

A bit of sun warmed my back. I had a sense of being fondly regarded, as in childhood by our mother. A mere physical sensation, and fleeting, yet it gave me comfort. I even glanced behind me. She wasn't there.

A man was clambering over the groynes. As he drew nearer, I saw it was Brine from the tourist information office. He looked thunderous – "Where is she?"

"Dunno," I said.

"If she don't come back soon, I'll offer the job around. Plenty would take it and be glad."

I hated him in my heart, and with reason. Not content with marking our few local buildings of interest on a handy street map, and directing visitors to the public toilets, he'd decided the town could do with a female figurehead. Something like Ilfracombe's Verity (but we couldn't afford Damien Hirst) or the French Lieutenant's Woman at Lyme Regis (nor Meryl Streep). He'd given Lucie the picturesque task. Put my sister on display. Made her traipse up and down the beach, displaying her charms. If he'd set out from the start to attract a violent sex offender, and thereby get us a spot on the news, he couldn't have done it better.

Day after day I loitered by the tideline, or wandered amid stranded jellies and unanchored rags of weed. Then trudging back to the promenade, I'd wipe the salt drops from my cheeks.

As I plodded homewards on a drear Thursday afternoon, Brine accosted me again, jumping out from the pillbox, his favoured hide. "I've been thinking, maybe after all we don't need her. You can take her place – act the part of her abandoned, grief-stricken boyfriend. Of course you'll have to commit to a daily schedule..."

"Piss off."

A gawk of sightseers near the coin-op telescope appeared both fascinated by me and repelled. "That's him," one said. Cameras snapped like turtles. I knew this was Brine's doing, for who else but he would use soppy rumours to net the wet pound? Then I had a terrible thought – maybe he'd done her harm, even killed her? But I comforted myself, if so then surely he wouldn't be regaling visitors with wild tales. He wasn't stupid, just publicity-mad.

Yet he'd been importuning her, I knew. In a romantic sense, he was my rival. At the same time, I wasn't his. For brothers cannot be lovers.

Outside our house (in a narrow street, loomed over by our neighbour, whose gable wall streams rain on to our cracked slates) I hesitated. Afraid to go indoors, because if my sister wasn't there now, I feared she never would be again.

Booted feet on the table and a saucy grin. "Did you miss me?" I felt an impulse of rage. Understood why men murder women. Just to stop them flitting around.

"Been to see Mum."

I stood by the empty fireplace, rubbing my hands together and shivering. "Well you've lost your job."

"Didn't want it anyway."

"Fine. You won't mind starving, then."

"Don't be like that, Tom."

My anger spent itself in silence. Eventually I told her all what'd been going on. How Brine had cast me in the role of sorrowing sweetheart.

She looked thoughtful and said "That's quite clever of him really. People love a sad story. They'll be spending money in the shops, maybe staying over, eating cream teas. I'll bet the Squid's roaring."

So we got over the awkwardness – or maybe she never

felt any. She chattered on – "Mother says the problem is by the sea it's all tragedy and loss and romantic despair. Night and day. And all year round, except maybe for the August Bank Holiday weekend. But she's more pragmatic. Says her nature's that of an inland person, not a dweller by the coast."

"She had no business leaving us," I said.

"I think she'd be really pleased if you'd visit her."

"No chance."

"Oh Tom. You've turned from a sad boy into a rigid man."

That night we both lay awake each side of the parting wall. Then I heard her breathing change and knew she was gone into far-wandering dreams. I remembered how when I was a boy lying in the loft under the skylight the moon seemed like a woman bending to gaze on me, so close and tenderly attentive I might almost reach and touch her face.

Stepmother

Although he didn't exactly choose me, I was a good housekeeper, found adequate to fill his ex-wife's position. Make do and mend. But the kids flew and clung to me, like nails to a magnet. Poor ugly little rejects; I found pity to be no weak emotion. Then I gave birth to my own child, he suckled at my breast. The scrawny kids hung around our Madonna-and-son tableau. I must love this baby, I told myself. But love didn't come naturally.

Sister Joy and the Spider

Creation myths from around the world: insight into other cultures and beliefs. The course was a requirement of the National Curriculum and rather hastily scrambled together by Sister Joy, using bits of stories off the internet.

'Biliku was the goddess of the north-east monsoon. She was violent and unpredictable – sending beautiful weather if she was in a good mood, or piling up storm clouds and hurling thunderbolts and lightning. She created the earth and hung it in the sky. She often took the form of a giant spider.' Sister Joy consulted the search engine's translation. *Darkly and terribly and very fast it moves loudless, their watchful eyes escapes nothing and nobody. Before the world became to create at all, wob Biliku already their nets and moved by the far empty night. And created with its large feelers the earth and hung it in the sky.*

'According to another legend, Biliku was the jealous possessor of fire, which a kingfisher stole from her while she was asleep. So Biliku hurled a pearl shell and cut off the bird's wings and tail, making the first man.

'But then after creating man and his environment she grew bored – unlike God who so loved the world – yes

Amy, what are you muttering? – and she returned to the sky.'

But humans live further in constant fear of her terrible rage outbreaks…

A very small spider dangled near Sister Joy's glasses, then landed on her page of notes. Excusing herself to the girls, she left the room with it.

She'd never abandoned a class before.

She watched the spider clamber through blades of grass.

She asked herself, what am I doing here?

Back in the classroom, Gemma Bingham was drawing a spider's web on the cover of her rough book.

'What do you imagine heaven is like?'

'Oh, a very beautiful rural landscape. Like south-west Ireland. Fuchsias growing wild. And the sea. I suppose that's everyone's idea of heaven.'

'Not mine,' said Sister Joy. 'I imagine a spider's web hung with dew drops.'

Sister Roma, perturbed: 'And what would we all be, the flies?'

The blood jiggling in her veins kept her awake. A horrible agitation, like being in love, but worse. Like Paul on the road to Damascus, blinded by the light of God, sprawling in the dust. Converted.

Above the altar, a stained-glass lamb carried a flag of St George. The grass so green, the cross so red, the peculiar symbolism. Sister Joy looked up and around the chapel – no spiders. Did they dislike the incense, the high singing voices, the Christianity? Might that splodge be one, perhaps? No…

Old Sister Wanda poked her in the back with a hymn book. She tried to refocus on the liturgy. Boring. She'd always loved the psalms, but now even these – all righteousness and the destruction of enemies. For I thy God am a jealous God. Thou shalt have no other God but me. Why not? – Sister Joy thought. Why should He be the only one?

The girls lingered around diplodocus in the central hall of the Natural History museum. Did he carry his tail straight out, or let it trail on the ground? Sister Joy walked on alone. The arachnids beckoned.

A forest scene behind glass. How many arachnids lurking in this small area? She pressed one of three buttons – correct, eighty-seven thousand! The world might almost be composed of spiders. A fantastically successful species, they will outlive Armageddon. Nuclear radiation doesn't bother them.

Strange that young people are always more interested in dinosaurs.

She found another spider in a high corner of the nuns' sitting-room, with its ball of babies on the verge of hatching. Seeing her, it sprang into the attack position. A clear threat was issued, a challenge. And she was moved by the spider's courage, its determination to protect its offspring. If only God had loved the world like that.

The carpets – perhaps they might charitably be regarded as rugs, since at no point did any of them meet a wall. Dust had worked into the ancient cord. The walls, dirty magnolia woodchip. It's terribly unsatisfactory, Sister Joy thought. Monasteries are clean and bare, austere, beautiful in their austerity. Convents are a mess. This one is, anyway.

She felt like apologising to the spider. 'The Daughters of Biliku deserve better than this,' she said aloud.

'The what?'

'I mean, the Order of St Bertilla.' But Sister Ellen continued to look at her strangely.

A great web, swaying as she crossed it. Soft notes, plink

plink, a heavenly xylophone. Then came Biliku.

She rides the wind, she hurtles in the storm. She captures her prey and eats it, she has no mercy. Her knees are jewelled and the stalks of her eyes like palms. Toothless she chatters.

Sister Joy woke up just in time. I might have died.

She thought: It was a nightmare.

She thought: It was a religious experience.

Sister Joy was asked to attend 'a little meeting'. And told it was 'nothing to worry about'.

A room of anxious eyes, all fixed on her. She'd been behaving a bit – she seemed a little – Did she have something on her mind?

No, Sister Joy replied, she was fine.

Well, they were all glad to hear that. But –

'Oh dear,' said Sister Bridget. 'A spider.'

'Not another one.'

'It's a perfect plague.'

The spider came marching across the carpet, heading in Sister Joy's direction.

'Someone put it out of the window.'

'They give me the shivers.'

'I'll deal with it,' said Sister Wanda. 'I'll fix its gaff.' And with surprising strength for a 92-year-old, she lifted a copy of the Authorised Version of the Bible, the weight of several bricks, high above her head and dropped it. 'Gotcha!'

'Be careful, it might run out from underneath…'

Sister Joy fainted.

The reason being, she'd nearly leapt from her chair and strangled Sister Wanda. *But humans live in constant fear of her terrible rage…* The effort not to, the inner conflict, had knocked her out.

Two weeks in bed with 'stress'. Any spiders were thoughtfully removed from her cell, since she obviously didn't like them.

Afterwards, life seemed drained of meaning. She continued going through the motions, but found she didn't believe in anything. She could no longer take delight in thinking of the huge mythical spider who *created with her feelers the earth and hung it in the sky.*

It wasn't till Easter that her faith returned, with the story of the resurrection and the stone rolled away from the door of the sepulchre. Sister Joy read of how Jesus appeared to Mary Magdalen and the disciples. The she returned by herself to the dark and empty tomb, and saw the web, a glittering miracle spanning the void. And the spider, waiting.

Seagull

After my sister lost her house in the divorce she moved to live with me, bringing with her a change of clothes and a book of Anglo-Saxon poetry. When not asleep on the sofa, she read The Wanderer or The Seafarer (he chooses the harsh life of the sea over a land of dead pleasures where there are no givers of gold) and watched seagulls floating over the rooftops. At least they're free, she sighed. So I wasn't surprised when one day I came home from work to find she'd gone. A gull swooping past cried farewell.

Teeth and Hair

The teeth sat on Mr Hitchcock's upturned palm like a joke, as if they might start talking by themselves. But Mr H is a funeral director, not a ventriloquist.

'This won't do, Miss Pilgrim. Stealing or purloining or otherwise abstracting a client's property.' Mr H always calls the dead people our clients. I asked him once, aren't their living relatives really our real clients? Them! he said, no. They just pay the bills.

'What d'you want with these? Eh?' He'd caught me popping them in my bag, just as I was going for lunch. 'Plastic teeth, Miss Pilgrim. That's all they are, you know. Acrylic. Cheap stuff. Worthless. Fetch nothing.'

'I wasn't going to...' I wanted to explain, it was the rat man. I didn't want him stealing people's teeth. We're sort of related, though I hope not by blood, he's a third cousin at most. But I didn't want to tell Mr H this, or any of it. Privacy is so important, he's always saying, even in death, Miss Pilgrim. Especially in death. Hence the expression, silent as the grave.

He's like that himself, I mean private. For instance, after he went to Torquay. Did you enjoy your holiday? I asked. He replied, it was sunny for at least half the week. And here? The same, I said, it was the same here. Torquay often gets better weather than Margate, he said. More sun, it being on the south coast proper.

From Mr H I learned that talking about the weather isn't shallow or pointless. It's a way of reassuring the other person, while keeping yourself separate.

Hitchcock and Dwell, it says in faded gold letters over our shop – what Mr H calls the establishment. Mr Dwell is dead. His name is really Dowell, the signwriter made a mistake and so they only paid half. But now he's Mr Dwell, for ever and ever. Or until we get a new sign. Maybe Hitchcock and Pilgrim, one day. I think Mr Hitchcock likes my name and wouldn't object to see it painted alongside his own.

After the teeth incident, I was so upset, I sat crying on the promenade, on a bench next the telescope. A man came and put 20p in for a go. What did he expect to see? The horizon. Mr Hitchcock's wife left him years ago, he refers to her as the first Mrs Hitchcock, although there's not been a second. Once he asked me, had I ever 'entertained thoughts of marriage?' Oh Mr Hitchcock, I said, I'm too young for all that. I'm only seventeen. He told me, in some countries and in historical times that would be old. You'd be on the shelf, at seventeen.

The rat man said, 'She done a runner. She ran off.' I don't want to know, I said, that's a private matter, between them. Anyway, it's all in the past. But I imagine her sometimes, in running shorts and trainers. I see her dashing along the promenade, then across the sand – making it spurt up – and leaping over the groynes. On and on she runs, around the coast of England, then Wales and Scotland.

Nothing is truly over and done with except when people die and not always then.

Between the funeral parlour and the sea are a lot of hotels, most are just family houses converted into B&Bs, with strings of fairy lights outside. Old people come in coaches down here from Yorkshire. They waltz very slowly around the ballroom of the Alhambra hotel. Some never go home again. They are delivered to us wrapped in nasty nylon sheets.

I would have to tell Mr H the truth, in order to exonerate myself. The rat man – he was a ratcatcher, then he got taken on by Thanet Council as a superior kind of dustman, paid extra to be discreet. 'No money in rats,' he said. While Mr H was in Torquay, he tried to corrupt me. 'The bags are round the back,' I said – he'd come in at reception.

Then he started to talk in such a peculiar way, I thought he might be having a stroke, or gone a bit loony. 'What?' I said.

'Rings.' As if *I* was stupid. 'It's rings I'm after.'

'There's a jeweller's in the shopping centre. On the ground floor, just past...'

'Off the corpses.'

My fingertips left sweat marks on our pictorial brochure of luxury headstones. But I managed to tell him, quite calmly, we give all personal effects back to the clients' relatives.

Dusty white blind, empty metal flower holder. While Mr H was on hols, I was thinking how I could smarten up our window display. Hitchcock and Pilgrim. I'd got some ideas.

Mr Butt was there when I got back. He and Mr H were drinking the whisky that we keep for the clients' relatives. And from the cut-crystal glasses. Mr H fixed me with a mournful stare, I wondered what it meant. Mr Butt was talking about the atrocious state of the property market, how he ought to have kept on being an air traffic controller, for the salary. He had a breakdown, Mr H told me. Houses don't zoom around like planes, they're not coming at you from all directions, little lights filled with people. But now often he complains to Mr H, 'They're not moving.' But that's Margate for you. People around here don't have money. He chose the wrong area to be an estate agent.

I said hello and walked past into the chapel of rest. One of our clients was there, a lady who used to live nearby. It was her teeth I'd taken, Mr H having arranged the face to look natural, using cotton wool and cardboard. He removes the teeth, because of shrinkage.

She was quite old, maybe in her seventies, but not decrepit. I'd done her make-up. And since she lived locally, I wondered if my friend Marianne ever washed her hair. She works at Roots & Tips, where they mainly get old ladies. She combs back their wet hair from their naked faces. One old girl, she always comes to find Marianne at the back of the shop, after she's tipped the hairdresser, to give her £1. She's nice, Marianne says, they all are really, even Mrs 'The water's too hot, the water's too cold'. Giving them rinses – 'Mind you don't get soap in my eyes.' Marianne says, 'I like sweeping up the mixed hair, it's dreamy. I love white hair.'

Mr H beckoned to me from the door, saying my name. He closed it behind me, as if the client might be listening. 'That earlier incident,' he said, 'was out of character, for one usually so trustworthy. I shouldn't have left you here alone, Miss Pilgrim, while I was on holiday. It was putting too much responsibility on young shoulders.'

'Oh Mr Hitchcock, please let me explain –' But he held up his hand. 'No need. We've both been under stress, Miss Pilgrim, owing to pressure of work. Our business is growing rapidly in the current recession and I need a partner to replace Mr Dowell.'

The air fluttered in my throat like a dove. I could only manage to say 'Yes?'

'And so I have asked Mr Butt to join me.'

'Mr Butt?'

Oh!

'He has accepted my proposal.'

If I'd told him – if he'd given me the chance – how I'd been approached by the rat man and not succumbed to temptation – but no, that wouldn't have made any difference.

'One needs capital to enter a partnership, Miss Pilgrim,' he said – guessing the truth, to my shame. 'And you're not quite mature enough. But one day, perhaps…'

I'd been deceiving myself and now everybody could mock me. Even the teeth of the nice old ladies would laugh – ha ha ha! Like I saw the rat man laughing in the public bar of the White Hart, making a show of the teeth he'd stolen. 'I say, I say, I say…' His mate pointed at me over his shoulder. So then I knew, I knew I had to do something. It felt like my responsibility. I decided not to tell Mr H. That was my mistake, perhaps.

Hitchcock and Butt!

Teeth are intimate. Since around the time of Mr Hitchcock's big disappointment, his holiday before last on the Solway coast, I've been trying to protect them. Remains of mouths, of kind smiles and loving kisses. The suitcase under my bed won't close now.

A man is standing outside Roots & Tips, in the lamplight and the falling rain. A chancer, a deceiver, a bit of a bully, I can tell just from the way a person stands. Waiting for whoever-she-is. But the shine of the lamp, in the rain, says she don't want him, it's like she's refusing. I almost frighten myself sometimes. Caring for the dead, see, that's what does it.

Out comes Jen the salon manager, used to be a goth with exploding hair, now it's purple. The old ladies don't mind experimental, only not on themselves.

Jen tells him to f– off. He slams the car door.

Inside the salon it's warm and light-hazy. One of them is complaining about how her scissors aren't sharp enough.

A woman's head is wrapped in silver. Now Jen takes off her coat, I see she's pregnant. It must be nice when it's not shameful. That whole secret world inside of you, a new creature being formed in the living fluid and protected while it grows, you needn't say anything, people know just from the shape of you.

They know.

But do they know anything, really? They can see you're pregnant, but not what it means to you. That's a secret you can never tell.

Men keep secrets too, nasty ones often. For instance, Marianne says that chap's her cousin and she was round visiting her aunt's house, she'd gone upstairs, then he called her from his room to just come in here a moment. I've got something to show you. He's a policeman, still living at home. And he said try this on you for size, like he was joking. It was a pair of handcuffs. I didn't know how to refuse politely, Marianne says. That's what she's like. Brought up to be nice to people and a bit stupid, only in the way she can't protect herself.

The air smells of mint, Jen is spraying her feet through her black tights. Hairdressers are like nurses, having to stand all day. I'm lucky. Marianne says, I just pulled my hand through and escaped – making a circle of her other hand to show. Otherwise – well. He was trying to lock me to the bedpost. But then I'd have screamed, so Auntie Mary would come upstairs. But I'd be so embarrassed.

My hand slipped through like a fish and I laughed. Can't catch me!

'You ought to tell someone.'

The old ladies are all gazing at themselves in the mirrors. Hoping they'll be turned young again. Would I sacrifice myself for one of them, like if she offered me a lot of money and her house in exchange for her being young and me being old? I think yes, I would. So long as I could go on living to enjoy the money, for at least sixty years. On an old-age pension. But that's not much. Anyway, for sixty years I'd be paying into a funeral insurance fund, so then I could have a mausoleum, black marble and stained glass windows. And six black horses to pull my hearse, with tall nodding feathers on their heads.

In between the pop songs comes the news. Millions of gallons of oil are escaping from a shipwrecked tanker off the coast of Spain, it's the world's biggest ever environmental disaster. Michael Jackson dangled his baby over a balcony. A man blew up his wife's car with a home-made bomb. A woman's dismembered limbs have been found in a canal and on allotments. The firefighters are going on strike.

One of the girls holds a little bit of dark red liquid in a bottle. Turned upside down it's a bottle of blood. I feel sick and we go outside. It's not raining. Marianne smokes a cigarette and she offers me one. It stops you vomiting. 'That's why I started,' Marianne says. 'When I was fourteen. I used to be so nervous. Oh Janie, hair is weird, it's like a living creature. I heard of a woman who died when she was quite young and she had red hair down to her shoulders. But by the time they dug her up, there was enough to stuff a sofa.'

'Why did they do that – open up her coffin?'

'To see if she'd been murdered.'

'I might do that,' I said. 'I'm getting bored with my job. There's always openings. I might train to be a specialist.' That word made me think of the rat man. I dismissed him from my mind. I thought of me organising the police, the gravediggers, the lights so they could work at night, the refreshments etc and the van for transferring the remains to forensics. I'd have my own vans, I'd be a company, Pilgrim & Pilgrim. With my daughter. I'd get her back.

Meanwhile I should rid myself of those teeth. They'd frighten her. I should let them go, maybe in the sea. I thought they'd look just like the skeletons of sea creatures. Could be embarrassing though, if the tide washed them all up. I should bury them down deep. In the dark, I walked along the promenade. I saw a bunch of sacking; no it was a person on the sand. Dead? But by the time I got down there, he'd roused himself. A fringe of beard around his pale face. He'd been looking in the sky for the bright dust of meteors, the lions. Except unfortunately it was too cloudy. Sit down with me. He pulled the band from my hair. Do you mind, I said, not really angry. He said, it's like a waterfall of honey. Sticky, I thought, and said out loud I never meant it to grow. I'm having it cut soon. But it's lovely, he said. I didn't mind when he touched me, I thought I'm loosening my bonds. He put a ring on my finger, of bone, of shell. Now you're married to the sea. I'll stay on dry land, thank you.

A jogger ran past and funnily enough she looked a bit like my idea of the first Mrs Hitchcock. When would she ever stop running? Maybe she was addicted to the amphetamines or the hormones, or whatever it gives you. Then I remembered my bag and slipped my hand inside, to check for the teeth. Mr H had given them back to me, like a kind of consolation prize. I know, I know, Miss Pilgrim. We'll say no more about it.

'What d'you think I've got in here?'

'Pearls.'

Mourning Angel

The mourning angel we installed on our mother's grave is like a crying doll, only 6ft high. Tears are piped through holes in her bronze eyes, from a storage tank fixed under her wings at the back. This tank didn't have much capacity, so my brother ran a T off the pipe to the cemetery tap, adding a solar-powered pump. Now on sunny days instead of dribbling down her face the tears shoot upwards and fall in a sparkling shower on the gravel path.

Small Tall

The famous author was lying under a tree at the Small Wonder short story festival, in a crumpled linen jacket. His bony intellectual nose resembled my brother's. His bony intellectual toes wriggled in the sun, free and enjoying it. His novel about a guilty woman writer had been shortlisted for and almost won the Booker Prize. It was the People's Choice that year. They asked him on TV how he felt about being the People's Choice. He said it was very gratifying.

His shoes (no socks) were placed together by the tree trunk. My feet slipped beneath their supple tongues, into their open throats. Too big at first, they shrank to fit. I tied the laces. Well shod for perhaps the first time, off I trotted.

They were beautiful brown leather shoes. Creased, not new, but quality. And now stolen, walked off with. But I didn't feel responsible. The shoes I felt were the true culprits, I their prisoner. They'd snatched me and were now hurrying me away to – where? I didn't have the least idea.

Then an audience was clapping as the shoes walked me into a marquee and pranced me up on stage. A book was thrust into my hands – who by, the shoes? I think so, but how could they? Of course they couldn't. What have shoes to do with hands?

But let me warn you now, shoes are powerful beings. Don't ever underestimate a shoe. Think of all that glue and stitching.

I started reading aloud from the book by the famous author. Who I wasn't, but nobody seemed to mind or notice. Some front-row faces looked a little puzzled, but willing to go along with it. Others were thoughtful, dreamy, listening. Yet somebody, or bodies, in the tent disliked me. I could taste their hatred at the back of my mouth like a dead animal, a sheep with it eyes pecked out. Sweat-infused, leathery malignity. Some plastic there too.

The author's muscly sentences and virile paragraphs continued to roll forth. (The genius of the man! Why had I never noticed it before?)

Who were these hidden things, polished yet festering? Shoes! The shoes of the well-disposed, civilised audience. They loathed me. However I'd now served the book's purpose. Hands went up, but the shoes wouldn't stay for questions. A woman kicked me as I passed, or her Birkenstock did. 'I'm terribly sorry,' she said. 'My foot must have gone to sleep.'

Wivelsfield, Haywards Heath, Gatwick Airport, East Croydon... The shoes were really hurting me by now. I undid the laces. They tied themselves up again. Pinch, bite – elegant torturers. Yet I couldn't help admiring them; noticing, for instance, the little frills between the vamp and the toe-box.

I was desperate to escape. The only person I could think of was my granny, who'd died long before.

Maybe Auntie Mary was still alive? I took a tube to Arnos Grove, first underground then overground, a lot of stations, in agony. They'd widened the track. The ruins of my granny's house peeped through the sycamores.

Getting inside was easy, somebody having torn the

front door off its hinges. Maybe the same person who'd lit a fire on her sitting-room carpet. Ashes and dust. Rotten floorboards. No sign of Auntie Mary. Unless –

The flicker of a tail, which vanished into a hole by the skirting board. 'Through here!' someone squeaked. I didn't think I possibly could, but then...

The place behind the skirting board was cosy and cluttered. I recognised my granny's furniture – a wardrobe, a glass-fronted display cabinet. And here was Auntie Mary, bright-eyed and long-tailed.

A red council tax form on the table. She'd scrawled across it, 'I am A MOUSE! Not legally obliged to pay taxes! Please amend your records!'

'You'll be safe in here, Ninnie. Shall I make you up a bed in the spare room? Are you fleeing anybody in particular?'

'Oh Auntie Mary,' I sobbed, 'my feet. It's these shoes.'

She fished a pair of old reading glasses from a drawer and peered through them. 'What very ugly shoes. Green, the colour of growth and gangrene.' My aunt herself was not wearing any shoes, or clothes.

'They belong to a famous author,' I said. 'He nearly won the Booker Prize.'

'That's all a lot of nonsense to me, my dear.'

'But look – ' I pointed to the little frills.

'Indeed,' she said. 'Are they cheap frills?'

'Certainly not!' I cried, outraged on the shoes' behalf.

'You should have walked a mile in them right away. It's too late now. What a predicament. I could try nibbling them off your feet, but then I might nibble your feet off too.'

Then: 'Oh, but of course,' she said. 'Why didn't I think of that in the first place? Pop back through the hole and presto, you'll expand to fit the human space available. Next, ask me for permission to come in again. This time I'll say, leave your shoes at the entrance. So they'll stay large, hopefully, while you diminish.

'But mind,' she warned me, 'as soon as you feel the shoes coming loose, kick them off and away from you. Otherwise who knows what might happen, it could be terrible.'

'Oh. OK then.'

I went outside and grew huge. 'May I come in?' I called.

Nose and whiskers. 'Of course you may, Ninnie. Certainly, my brother's child, my fresh new self, come take my place at the table, eat my food and drink from my glass. But first, please remove your shoes and leave them at the door.'

As I telescoped, the shoes yawned. I managed to kick one off before sinking into the other. It was big as the Grand Canyon. No, I exaggerate. Some other canyon, more modest in scale, attracting fewer tourists.

Auntie Mary perched on the edge and called down: 'Ninnie, Ninnie, grab hold of my tail!' It felt springy like a snake. I hauled myself to safety, or into daylight anyway.

One of the dreadful shoes lay on its side, the other sat upright. I rubbed my feet – pins and needles – while my aunt scuttled around. 'They might be converted into flats, or even maisonettes. I have a friend,' she said, 'the mother of a large family, including five great greedy adolescent boys who refuse to leave home. She may well be interested.'

Marriage Counselling

Marriage counselling turned out to be a bad idea. For instance, one week my husband mentioned his love of sailing, this being a point of friction between us. The next week I happened to notice Jean our counsellor was wearing deck shoes and a breathable gilet, her hair tied up jauntily with knitted string. The air tingled, shot with bright particles of attraction. I want a divorce, I said, but they both ignored me. Their joint idiocy released me from the guilt of my own marital blunders; I got up and left. Sharp black silhouettes of buildings against the blue January sky.

Watery

Because she's stopped believing the newspapers, she wants proof of America's existence. Because if only the bits of land she's seen for herself and trodden on are there, that doesn't include most continents. A world based on her own experience would be more gap than reality. So she needs proof. America is the test.

First she asked the heron – because it might have contacts, or esoteric knowledge. You never know with birds. The heron was hunting moles in the waterlogged field, but only finding pale, semi-dissolved worms. It paused with beak uplifted, musing, or perhaps gauging the hydroscopic atmosphere, then flapped off laboriously.

Next she asked the rain, whose nature was changeable. It had probably been to America a few times, via rivers and the ocean, and now here it was, back again, undermining things or removing them gradually or at once, e.g. walls, topsoil. But rain isn't malicious. It's a world-processor.

The rain said pitter patter, splish splash, downpour. And why is it so important.

I don't know, she said.

Fly from Newcastle to Belfast, the rain advised. To get a

visa. And you'll have to think of a good reason, or several. With a final sigh of avoid Nevada, try Mississippi, the rain shrank into a cloud and stopped.

But, she said.

Water roars down the culvert, by the side of the house. This too was rain, falling on the fells, drenching copses and flooding old mine workings. Now it's here, now gone, off to join the little South Tyne, the big Tyne, the North Sea. Cold to swim in, despite a one-degree rise in temperature. Horse riders on the beach. A man pointed to a line on a chart, then flew to give his environmental talk in another city. He didn't mention plane emissions. He recommended low-energy lightbulbs. She's tried them, but her eyesight is poor. In the 1930s there was a double nettie over the culvert. That puzzles her – how would it work? The culvert dries up in summer. She has a septic tank (that doesn't really work either). But other times – last week, for instance, a wave of water came down from the field, knocked over the dustbin, filled her wellies in the porch, spread through the kitchen and exited via the sitting-room floorboards, on its way sousing a junction box; the electrician showed her where mice had nibbled the plastic, leaving bare wires.

So even if you leave things alone, they keep changing, inconstant. America is just a name, she thinks, while squatting to look more closely at earth, grass roots and tiny stones.

Catching Fire

The smallest things made him angry. He would light a fire in the cranky old woodburning stove and instruct her to keep it alive. But however hard she tried, the fire always went out, suffocated by its own smoke. Glancing through the window, she noticed a clump of snowdrops under the sycamore. Every year they took her by surprise. A fluttering distracted her, was it in the garden or the field, or – she pressed a hand above her belly, felt it, invisible but here. Would she tell him? No, she decided. And knew she must leave this place.

The People Before Me

The people before me, the ones who sold me this house, only stayed a year. Although they'd planned to renovate extensively and for this to be their dream home, something interrupted them and changed their plans. So they returned the floor sander to the hire shop, left tins of Dulux almost unused and walls half-papered. They contacted estate agents, put the house back on the market and while waiting for it to sell, they moved in with her sister.

But this house never felt abandoned. To me it felt loved. This house had inspired love in some other unknown person, a quiet power I could sense in the hallway, on the stairs, in all the rooms. I asked my neighbours, who lived here before the people before me? An old lady, they said, a spinster, who kept herself to herself and was a bit peculiar and brisk, but very nice. She lived in your house for decades. She wore men's clothes, trousers and waistcoats.

Listed in the deeds, I found Nora Fielding. Perhaps she'd died in this house, leaving her photographs and ornaments, certificates and savings books, clothes and underclothes, all her earthly remains. I felt jealous of whoever – maybe the person before me? – had cleared the house.

Nothing left of her now. Except.

I am thinking about everything I've lost and trying to conjure it back to me, but the words I'm putting down and crossing out don't help, they're just a list of former possessions and loves. I sigh, as I often do sigh when I'm writing, and glance up, to see her standing beside me. Young and slender, wearing tailored men's clothes. She's looking down at me with a half-smile, in a teasing, intimate way. The shock of her is like drinking red wine on an empty stomach. My heart beats in my ears. Now nothing separates us one from the other, her from myself, and I know I'll never change anything. The people before me don't really exist, they are like ghosts or just memories.

Blackbird

One day, Linda was sitting on her kitchen doorstep when a blackbird spoke from its perch on a flowering branch of the apple tree. "Worro mate," it greeted her. "Ow bist?"

"Ah'm feelin like two penn'orth of God help me," Linda said.

"Ar, yow do ave a fairce like a bosted boot."

Encouraged by this friendly sympathy, Linda told the bird all her troubles. The bills – she had to explain what a bill meant in this context – the debts and the son who never gave her a kind word. A moment later, this same son entered the kitchen and dumped his plate by the sink.

"Ah'm grateful for small mercies," Linda said once he'd gone.

"Lickle humiliations," the bird contradicted. "Worms i'the ticker. No, dow bless him or be grateful. Yow'm not his skivvy."

You may wonder why a bird talking to her in black country dialect, or any human language, didn't alarm Linda. The reason being she'd lived all her life in Rowley, where past and present often temporarily swap places, accustoming the inhabitants to magical events. For instance, when she was a child peeking out at night she'd seen fires burning all over the land, much like a vision of Hell. Black by day and red by night as an old saying describes the area. And aged thirteen, fleeing the persecutions of her bullying brother, afraid to go home, she'd found herself in a little country lane overhung by trees, a place she could never find again.

So Linda was glad of this opportunity to converse with a blackbird. Oh yes, he told her, many a time he'd sung in that country lane. "It ay there no more. And yet it be."

The bird preened itself, re-aligned an errant wing feather. "Give us some crumbs." Amused by its cheek, Linda threw crumbs on the grass and the bird flew down and pecked them up. "Now open yer winder, the one over the sink," it told her. A bit puzzled, Linda obeyed. Whereupon the virtuoso warbler sang a complicated phrase. A gust of wind blew a rain shower through Linda's kitchen window, scoured the dishes clean. Meanwhile in shone the sun and dried the plates and cups.

But while exiting via the same window, the wind unluckily dislodged a mug, which smashed on the quarry tiles. Her son's favourite, a big one embossed with Disney characters. Oh dear, oh dear. As Linda was sweeping the bits into her dustpan he came in and seeing his broken mug – "You stupid woman!" he flung at her. And she cowered from him, the boy she'd loved, now a grown man. Calling her stupid, like her dad whose name for her was Thickety.

Next morning the blackbird sang a piece of an ancient song: "Did yer think oi would lay down and doi, oh no, not oi..." It fluttered in the apple tree, then hopped about by the kitchen door.

"Stap yer ivverin an ovverin," Linda snapped. "Ah cor stond it."

The bird tilted its head. "Ah thought yow'd be proper chuffed ter see me."

"Well ah bay. Me lad's not spakin ter me an it's acos of yower clarting around, yow big lommock."

The bird was sorry to hear about the smashed mug and apologised for the wind's boisterous behaviour. "But chirrup, ower kid, fer ah'll grant yow any wish yer loike." It made a couple of suggestions, guessing at what might be Linda's heart's desire – a bank error in her favour? Golden apples – not Golden Delicious but made of real gold? As she was hesitating it told her to throw down some crumbs, which it ate in a businesslike fashion. "Ta. Now what's it ter be?"

"I just want me lad to show me a bit o'kindness," Linda said. "A bit o'saft. Like when e were a nipper. Forget ackers an diamonds, that's my wish."

"Granted," the bird said. "Trarabit, keep out th'oss road." It flew off.

10pm: Linda was in her coat and slippers, grilling herself a round of cheese on toast, when she heard her son's key in the front door. Home early from the Three Barrels. She tensed as he entered the kitchen, but his demeanour was changed. "Soz, Mom." He held out his hand as though offering it to a mistrustful cat or dog for them to sniff.

A clumsy embrace. "Yo'am awright, yo'am," he whispered in her ear and she felt herself blush at this declaration of filial affection. He pressed his lips against hers in a child's innocent kiss. But the kiss took itself further. They sprang apart, both horrified. He lamped her and she fell, striking her head on a corner of the oven. He didn't call an ambulance, or offer to take her to Accident & Emergency. Left her shivering and bleeding on the quarry tiles.

All night she lay there, until light pierced the sky and the blackbird uttered its first notes. Pulling herself shakily upright, she took the slice of hard toast with flabby cheese on it from the grill, tore it apart and threw it on the grass. The blackbird swooped down, but then, oh! – a cat pounced on the defenceless creature.

Linda shooed off the predator and raised the bird tenderly in cupped hands. It opened and closed its beak, its narrow tongue moved as if trying to speak. Her tears fell on its bloody breast. When it died her spirit left her body, flew and perched in the apple tree.

And if ever while walking in the vicinity of Curral Road, near the quarries, you should by chance find yourself in a sunken green lane of queer beauty, you may hear her singing: "Did yer think oi would lay down and doi, oh no, not oi..."

A Seduction

That summer, I was captured by a flash riptide, snaking in from the deep to net foolish amateurs, a pure but deadly line in the ruffled waters. As I struggled to swim shorewards, the ocean courteously insisted on taking me in quite another direction. It fancied a stroll to the horizon, twirling its jellyfish-like parasol. Would I be its new friend? Might we have a love/death affair? Luckily, I remembered some advice about escaping from riptides. You must swim crabwise, not straightforwardly but eluding definition, refusing to let yourself be fast-tracked. Like a line of writing going across the page, not like a woman so anxious to save her own life she can't think clearly and arrange words in grammatical sentences.

So with crafty persistence I refused the serpent's invitation, pleaded innocence, groped for the shallows, found my footing. But even then I wasn't let go. An overarching wave grabbed me and tumbled me about like sheets in a washing machine, I boiled in a swell of blue-green-white bubbles, and when it spat me out again I was walking upside down. Reverting to type, I saw children playing in the day's brightness, a sandy and sober-dry vision. The sea only had me in ankle chains when an old woman carrying a surfboard halted my progress. Excuse me, dear. Your left boob. I glanced down – there it was indeed. Pulling up my costume, I said thank you.

I Should Go Back to the Dance Class

I should go back to the dance class, even though I really don't want to. Recently, Danielle sent us an email about how it's spring and the birdies are tweeting, new leaves unfurling, sap rising, the whole of nature is joyful and she hoped to see us all at the dance class on Wednesday, 7pm at St Faith's church hall. It's an old Nissen hut, asbestos, with draughty metal windows and radiators like school ones.

There came a point in November, I just couldn't bear to raise myself from in front of the TV and plod down our street, then over the railway bridge and across the Great West Road. Or be late again, squeezing into my holey leggings while the rest of them are doing their limbering-up exercises. So I rang Danielle and because I'm honest, I didn't try and fob her off with an excuse. "I'm just finding it really hard," I said. In the background I could hear laughter and posh voices, glasses clinking and cutlery scraping, it sounded like *Come Dine With Me*, except I don't suppose Danielle ever watches that.

Anyway, she said if I truly needed to take a break then OK, but "Do please carry on doing the stretches and aerobic jumps. And of course, keep eating your five a day." Fruit and vegetables, she meant. Ha ha, I thought, because I've tried this and in my view it is impossible. Actually, I felt irritated by her nutritional advice. Still, it must've seeped into my unconscious mind, because recently I bought a chicken at Somerfield. And put it in the fridge.

"Cripes, this has nearly reached its sell-by date" – my husband. "Better chuck it out, or do something with it."

So I removed the plastic and slid a knife under the knobbly skin. It came away from the breast easily, but stuck to the thighs and knees. For some reason this put me in mind of Danielle, in her low-cut and high-cut leotard. She shows a lot of flesh, I say this just as an observation. Well, she's got no reason to be shy or ashamed. Not an ounce of orange peel. And she rolls on or strips off her woolly legwarmers with cool insouciance.

The skinning took ages as usual – I always forget, in the years between one chicken and another, how long it takes me. And how the white fat clings stubbornly to the pink flesh and when you break the bones at their joints you can see traces of blood, although not much. Shouldn't blood be pouring from the chicken's many wounds, dripping off the table, splattering the walls? But no, I suppose chickens do all their bleeding in the abattoir.

This chicken, I thought, was once a hen. A beautiful living creature. Now it's got no feathers or dignity. Beneath the ribs, a dark cavern. Although my organs have not been eviscerated, very often I feel hollow and empty. Chickens used to contain little plastic bags of giblets, like free surprise gifts – the bird making a present of its own insides. My mum boiled up the giblets to make gravy for our Sunday roast… Before I knew what I was doing, I'd wrenched open the back door and thrown the chicken, skin and all, into our yard. It bounced flabbily and landed near the fence. I thought, the foxes will be pleased anyway. It wasn't dark yet, but dark enough. The chicken would be gone by morning.

Bernard came into the kitchen and shook his head like a wet dog, as if to say, "I must've been imagining what I just saw happen." He filled the kettle, enough for two mugs. After he'd made tea and I was feeling calmer, we went back through. He took the broken side of the sofa, which seemed to me a kind gesture. I didn't despise him for it. We watched some advertisements.

I felt like having a conversation, so I asked him, "Are you ever afraid I might kill you?"

He laughed. "No, why would you do that?"

"For any reason. If I was in a bad mood."

"Thought you liked me."

That made me stop and think, was it true. "As much as I like anyone," I said at last. He seemed satisfied. But isn't that really what marriage boils down to? Once you're past the romantic stage. Married couples who are still lovey-dovey after 20 or 30 years, I find that distasteful. Don't get me wrong, I enjoy kissing, or I used to, but not now, with him, it would feel all wrong. Genital contact is different. Sex is just an automatic reaction.

He riffled through some takeaway leaflets. "I fancy a pizza." Just then, the doorbell rang. "That was quick."

With hindsight, it would've been more sensible just to ignore the bell. Although I was surprised to see Danielle standing outside, I politely asked her in. She had on pink leggings, a see-through mac and a sort of textile necklace that made me think of the bit of string they fasten around a chicken's trussed-up legs. Was she in fact the chicken, come back through the front door to haunt me? I blinked this thought away. Her hair was down, all crinkly blonde, and she had a tan – I remembered she'd been on a study visit to India.

"Janine" – she waved aside my offer of tea/coffee –

"I'm very concerned about your prolonged absence from the dance class. It shows a lack of motivation and energy. A poor self-image, resulting in self-neglect."

Bernie made a noise like a cough, or clearing his throat – his way of laughing while pretending he's not. He'd turned the TV volume down, to be hospitable, but was still gazing at the screen. Danielle avoided sitting down next to him by perching on our low glass table. The takeaway leaflets stuck out from under her bottom. "I feel a responsibility towards you, as your teacher," she said, "and Janine, I'm puzzled, you used to be one of my best students. What happened? You were always so keen to learn, you really made an effort… "

"Oh, I don't know," I said vaguely.

Her eyes went whoomph, like gas catching under a saucepan. "That's not good enough!"

Part of me wanted to say I'm sorry, it's me, I get enthusiastic about things and then just lose interest. I was the same at school and with one boyfriend after another… wish I could change… However, I also resented the way she was lecturing me and shouting at me. For fuck's sake, I thought, it's only a dance class. Out loud, I said "Danielle, is the dance class really that important to anyone, even you?"

She gazed at me with her mouth open. At last she said "You're right. It doesn't matter." She started crying. "Nothing does…" Bernard turned off the TV, a sign he was startled, and I sat down next to him.

She told us how her life was falling apart, because her husband had found someone else. And how cold he'd been towards her, even before he met this other woman. "It was dead long ago. You're lucky yours is still alive."

At first I was puzzled, then I realised she meant our marriage. "Well it's stable," I said, looking at Bernard.

"What? Oh yeah."

She asked how long we'd been together. Twenty-two

years, Bernard told her. It sounded a terrible amount, like a judgement on us, not something to be proud of. But, least he's never betrayed me. We were even holding hands, a fact of which I gradually became conscious. I didn't know who'd taken the other's hand first. That's another thing – a marriage does sometimes generate its own special moments and decisions. Both good and bad ones. A marriage is almost like a living thing, not just a container or an agreement. Which is maybe true of any sort of relationship, I don't know.

"If you need somewhere to stay, you can move in here," I told her. "That's a genuine offer, Danielle. I'll clear the spare room, it's still got a few of our daughter's things in…"

"Oh no, I couldn't possibly. But you've been so kind." She sighed and blew her nose. "I'd better go."

"Danielle, I know true love is somewhere out there waiting for you," I said on the doorstep.

"Is it?" Her voice was hopeless.

"You're still young. Believe me, your sell-by date's a long way off."

She gazed into the darkness. "Where do I go from here?" Of course I knew she wasn't literally asking for directions, because her home's just round the corner. But I offered her a lift in the car, which she didn't want.

Still worried after ten minutes, I phoned her and was relieved when she answered. "Who is this?"

"It's me, Janine."

"Who? Oh, Janine. It's quite late."

"Sorry, but – "

"However, I'm glad you rang." Her voice was like the icy smoke from a freezer cabinet. "It's about the dance class, presumably?"

"No, I just wanted to check you got home OK…"

"Oh yes. The dance class is tomorrow evening, 7pm at St Faith's." Click – and she'd cut me off. Leaving me numb and disbelieving. I just stood there, with the phone receiver in my hand, until at last I said "She was really rude to me."

"Maybe her husband was there," Bernard suggested.

"Yes, maybe," I said slowly. "That would account for it."

He went into the kitchen. "Ham or chicken sandwich?"

"Ham."

"Reckon I'll have chicken." Opening the fridge, he took out the ham – which is actually turkey, it says on the packet – and the tub of Coronation Chicken.

I wondered about the real chicken, had the foxes taken it yet. In fact I nearly opened the back door, the knob was in my hand, but I felt afraid – which I know must sound silly. It wasn't the foxes I was scared of, but a nightmare vision of the chicken itself. How it might come to life again as a beaked and feathered creature, and fly at me to peck my eyes out. Taking Nature's revenge. Or be naked, only half dead – or still half alive – and dragging itself across the yard towards the house. That's what I imagined. So instead I locked up and put the key among the knives, and closed that drawer tight.

On my way up to bed, I paused on the landing. Our double glazing is such a blessing, because that window above the stairs used to be really draughty. When we first came here it was single glass with coloured shields, I was sorry to say goodbye to them.

I mounted Bernard, then he got on top. Sometimes we do it in a different order, but apart from that our sex life hardly varies. It's been the same for years, a comforting routine. In a funny way this is what keeps me sane.

Be Wise

She listened to him in silence, wanting to shout and scream.
Be wise, she told herself. That night an oak blew down in
a storm, cracking but not breaking the patio windows. She
rang a clearance firm, they sliced up the tree and fed it into
a chipper. The marriage held, just.

Oxygen for a Minotaur

My feet hurt and my veins feel stodgy, the blood unwilling to move. I trudge through Shepherds Fold and past The Knights Quest, no apostrophes. Around the back of Roman Bathroom, no ess, I restore a stranded worm to a patch of earth near a skip. Just for spite I could just die, like a light switching myself off, to scare someone. Here's Lol Dolormundi's hair salon, a dry cut for only £3.50, I don't know how she pays the rent. Also wash and sets, and pulling hair through a cap. Here's the pharmacy with its automatic door, hard to get in but at least there's no queue at the counter. I whisper my request and the girl hesitates, then fetches the chemist in his white coat. He says: "I can give you a 3% solution. The 5% is for men only."

"I need extra strength. It's not for me, it's for my husband."

"And it's a topical medication," he stresses. "To be applied to the scalp, not taken internally."

"Yes. No."

The chemist has what's called a full head of shiny black hair. I don't think the opposite needs remedy, but that's just my opinion. Since his forcible retirement, Jim's become fixated on lack and emptiness.

Home again. I should chuck the bits of old dry seaweed that festoon – maybe too strong a word – our porch. As I'm thinking this, I become aware of Jim on the door's other side, waiting and breathing. The tension isn't romantic, but I can feel it and probably he does too.

While I'm still twisting my key in the lock, he pulls the door open. "Did you get the hair stuff?"

"Yes."

"Where is it, then?"

"Give me a moment." I sink into a chair. He plucks the carton from my bag and scurries off. This house is dark and the shadows can just eat you up, if you let them. Whenever I turn a light on, he switches it off again. To economise.

"Want a cuppa?" – his voice floats back. I croak acceptance. Many minutes later, I reach the kitchen. He's not there, but he's left me a cup of tea. The blue and white carton stands beside it on the table. Midoxil – i.e. oxygen for middle age, the remedy for an ailing marriage? But no, I'm wrong: it's Minoxidil. Oxygen for a minotaur, his pelt no longer glossy. Starved of light and air in his underground labyrinth. Dangerous all the same. This tea has an odd taste, I notice. It is undrinkable and not to be taken internally. After the first sip, I pour it down the sink.

Our Silence

We never exactly fell out, just stopped talking. However, we continued to live in our housing association flat; we had no option. They'd bunged us in together. "I could kill her," I told Diane, my niece.

"Seriously?" Diane gave me an alert look.

"She's so patronising and rude."

"Is she really?"

"Yes," I said, feeling uncertain. Diane's challenges tend to knock me off-balance.

"But – "

"You don't have to live with her."

Marcella entered the kitchen, in her usual guise of lovely warm person. Hair bouncing with gold highlights and designer high heels clacking on the lino. "Hello, Diane! How are things? How's your mum?" As she knew perfectly well, Diane's mother and I don't get on. My heart raged.

She filled the kettle – past the half-way mark – and switched it on. "That's far too much water," I said, "for just yourself." Then she offered Diane a "cuppa", but having received a polite no thank you, she did not tip any water out. She hummed a little tune while guarding the kettle.

"Are you two still having that same old argument about the kettle?" Diane said. "I can't believe it!"

Marcella replied, "Who's arguing?"

As soon as she'd left the room, carrying her Royal Wedding mug by its bone china handle, I emptied the kettle down the sink, then dried it inside with a tea towel. Otherwise limescale might form and clog the element, I explained to Diane. My vigilance had so far prevented this from happening.

"I can't bear seeing you like this," Diane said.

After she'd gone, I sat for a while at the kitchen table. The plane tree rattled its dry leaves. I thought of that long-ago duty visit to my sister. In my early twenties, I'd been teaching in Austria. She'd married and had a child. She opened the newly sanded and painted front door of their three-storey silk weaver's house in East London, and said "Hi". In her usual tone of faintly amused disdain. "Just put your coat..." She led the way through to a kitchen diner with French windows and a sitting area. "This is, you know" – She waved a hand vaguely – "your Aunt Louise," she told a sturdily built child holding a wand and dressed as perhaps a woodland nymph or tree spirit, all in brown with a green pointed felt collar.

Unsure what to say, I tried hello, then "Your hair is shiny like a conker".

The child bypassed my prattle. "You're late," she said. "I've been waiting more than a hundred years."

"Twenty minutes," my sister corrected.

"Because she, *this one*" – the child pointed – "is not my real mother. She is a made-up. And she tells fibs." My sister gave an edge-of-panic laugh. "So will you help me to escape?" the child persisted. No, I said. "Why won't you?"

"Because the police might arrest me and put me in jail."

"Then I'll make a magic" – her wand scribbled the air – "and BOOM!"

"She's over-excited," my sister said. "Come on, it's time

for your nap."

"I put a spell on you!" the child called back over her mother's shoulder. "Now you're my servant! You have to do whatever I say!"

Unexpectedly, I did feel bonded to her – on her side, with a conviction she was on mine. I liked how certain she seemed to be about everything. And she retained that core strength. She didn't grow to resemble my sister.

On her next visit Diane brought a second kettle, one with a gold-plated element to discourage limescale. This apparently would solve all our problems and make us friends again. But would it be economical and good for the environment, offsetting Marcella's habit of leaving already-heated water in the kettle, to be processed twice or three times? No. Marcella, though, was delighted. She exclaimed! She raved! She filled the kettle and plugged it in. So now it was 'her' kettle, at 'her' end of the worktop. And the old inferior kettle became mine.

I said nothing. And from then on, we simply ignored each other. It seemed a civilised way of managing our hostilities. If we happened to pass in a communal area, we gave no sign of recognition. Our eyelids may have flickered, but our eyes remained blank.

One morning – she's being very quiet, I thought to myself. I knew she hadn't left the flat that morning, and I'd heard her boiling the kettle for a nightcap. She must still be in her room. Perhaps she's overslept, I thought. Hours passed. I began to feel very disturbed.

Should I knock on the door? Call to her? But what would I say? Hello it's me, Louise, your flatmate. Sorry we haven't spoken for a while, but just thought I'd check, are you OK?

Nervously I approached her sanctum and put an ear to the polished pine. Turned the knob, went in. Only a bit of light filtered through the curtains. No sound of breathing. Although I told myself, she's a quiet sleeper…

Back in our hallway, I tried to ring Diane. The phone wouldn't work. Remembering I'd disconnected it from the socket because of nuisance calls (Marcella had just shrugged and bought herself a mobile) I plugged the lead in with trembling hands. "Diane? Is that Diane?"

Of course, I'd known Marcella was fragile – "heart condition," she'd said, patting her ribs, "that's what got me on the housing list" – but she was only in her sixties. It shocked me. I really mean that.

I'm in the cemetery – I don't know how much later. Time is a savage sea, huge waves dash me down, I glimpse the shore, lose sight of it again. Her hand in mine, I kissed her lips. Whispered I'm sorry. Please forgive me.

Clay is fresh-turned on her grave. The air's silence is disturbed by harsh cries of birds. I'm not speaking to her, even in my mind, but she feels close as never before. I hope she's accepted my apology. It all seems so petty now. I'm holding the kettle – her one, still half-full of water – and I look around for a plug point... but no... I meant to put flowers in the kettle, as a memorial gift for her. Damn, I forgot to buy any.

A voice says auntie. A woman and child are standing nearby. They are both Diane. "Which one is you?" I ask.

"This is Jemma. I'm Diane, your niece. Oh Auntie..." She touches my sleeve. The child runs off to play.

"Diane... you're pregnant?"

"It's been years. Why wouldn't you answer the phone, or ever come to the door?"

Yes, I think, Marcella did get a bit peculiar. And then she died. With all her hair spread over the pillow. "Marcella died."

"Yes."

"Did you know that?"

"Yes, because you phoned me. Dear Auntie, I don't think you can go on living in the flat by yourself."

She's right, of course. They'll want to put a family in.

Marcella won't like that.

"Would you come and live with us?" As I'm hesitating, the child runs back. Her hair is shiny like a conker. A pink plastic windmill is gripped in her little fist. "Oh, Jemma! Did that come from a grave? You mustn't take something that belongs to – "

Brandishing the windmill, the child shouts at her mother, "The little girl said I could have it, to make magic spells!" She points it at me – "Whoosh, now you're alive!"

The Hairs on my Chinny-chin-chin

However many times I applied the facial hair remover cream and for however long, it remained bog useless. It did nowt but make my chin red, leaving the bristly hairs alone. We sat there cackling and blaming EU regulations. But Granny Smith – I turned to the oldest of our number – you could blast my chin hairs using your patented purée of withered carrot and mouldy turnip, at the sickle moon. She replied, of course I could. But as witches, aren't our hooked-nose, hairy, wrinkled old faces basically our shop windows? If we stop being ugly, who will take us seriously?

Rabbit On

On my return, I noticed men carrying power equipment from our house. One gave me a sympathetic glance, as though he knew things I'd soon find out for myself.

Sure enough – a hole in our living room wall, disrupting the division between our house and next door, hers. We'd been knocked through, without my permission.

Dusty TV and furniture, dusty kids (who stood transfixed in the swirling air like watchers by the gates of a demolition site), even the rabbit was dusty. My husband – also dusty, but haloed by hallway light – materialised in the new portal and clambered over a pile of smashed bricks. Get whatever things you'll need, he told the kids, while Mum and I have a chat.

What the eff have you done, I cried, thinking of our insurance policy. Then he grinned a foolish grin and my brain's tiny digits clicked into place. It's a trial run, he said. Minimum disruption to both our lives. She's not sure yet about Us.

By Us/both, he meant him and her.

Single in our double bed that night, I mentally replayed the scene of my kids' departure, watching them troop through the hole over and over, little soldiers. I remembered my own childhood, when told off for self-pity I learned to be stalwart. Not so different from me after all.

The rabbit lay on my throat and breast, an unexpected comfort. Oh rabbit! My tears fell on its still-grimy fur and I resolved to wash it properly in the morning.

Idiot, why didn't you notice and put a stop... So I accused myself as the moon restlessly glided between window panes. In contrast to which and its usual rabbit self, the rabbit hardly moved. I felt anchored by it, in a good way. At last it shifted, as though considering how best to advise me. Then it spoke, not exactly aloud, though I did hear a whiskery whisper, but as if – gently, not using its claws – it had tunnelled a way into my heart. Information gathered at this early stage may prove useful in the divorce courts, it said.

Early, I sobbingly sniffed. They might've been carrying on for months, years!

No, it's a recent development, or I'd have noticed – I keep my ears up. No suspicious signs until after we came back from holiday. The rabbit spoke inclusively because we'd taken it with us to Devon. Although as you may recall, it added, he frequently left the cottage, absenting himself for half an hour or more.

Because he needed to keep in regular phone contact with his office, I said. A major project...

How naïve you are.

The holiday hadn't been an easy one: quarrelling kids, taciturn husband. Swimming in a safe-seeming place, I was thrown on the rocks by a wave. My leg scabbed but then got infected and refused to heal; it was still a bit twingy.

Never mind, the rabbit said. You may have lost him and the kids – temporarily – but the important thing is, you've still got me. And I have a plan. I'll spy on them unnoticed, because who would suspect a rabbit, and feed you regular updates.

But he's boarded up the hole, I objected. From their side, I mean her side.

Trust me. I know another way in.

At first light out I crept, guilty burden partially hidden under my coat. Down the garden to a place where the rabbit could easily tunnel under the fence, as it often does, failing our efforts to escape-proof the area. Watching it lollop up her path, I remembered the last time she'd passed the rabbit back to me over this same section of fence. One of its paws was bleeding. Her lettuces nibbled to stumps in their raised beds. I took delivery and held the rabbit close. Its eyeballs rolled, I felt its rapid heartbeat on my bare arm. I'm so sorry, I said, and she replied, OK can't be helped. For a moment it seemed she knew, what? – everything about me – and understood. Mother-figuring, a bad old habit of mine. I yearned for something deeper than her kind willingness to forgive/overlook rabbit trespass and theft. Though I did appreciate that. Also I envied her jeans and jacket: good material, not programmed to self-destruct like my cheap cottons bundled in with family washes.

Red dawn: I surreptitiously watched the rabbit's progress. It paused by my neighbour's back door, which is fitted with a cat flap, why I don't know, and twitched an ear in salute. As if to say, I'm going in! Oh brave rabbit, my friend in adversity. We've been together a long time, ever since my first rabbit vanished, probably taken by a fox, and at the kids' insistence, though as Rabbit 1's primary caregiver I felt far from ready to buy a replacement, off we went to the pet shop. Here I practised a simple deception on my offspring to sway things in favour of a brown rabbit, telling them all the black-and-white ones and the albinos had been reserved by other families.

This same deft and clever rabbit – good choice! – hopped hitchlessly through the cat flap. Vanished from sight.

To begin with I trusted the rabbit absolutely, but after a few days I started to have doubts. Keep the faith! Meanwhile my husband would creep around the house, usually 2am to 4am, hoping not to wake me. I'd get up and scream at him and clutch air as he ran for the door in the party wall – for a new hinged door had replaced the boards – en route scattering clothes, toiletries etc.

Although despicable, I knew he wasn't the real enemy. She, my rival for everyone's affections, maybe even the rabbit's, lurked in her lair. At 8.45am when she left for work – she owns a bridalwear shop, ironically – I'd gaze from my top window like a bottled spider. She'd lift her hair out from under her coat's furry collar and walk off quick quick, hair floating behind.

Getting the kids back was easier than I'd imagined. One chilly Saturday morning, starlings twittering on the aerials, I waited till she'd gone out then tried the door and found it wasn't locked. Stepping over a dangerous gap, I crossed the boundary. Bit late in the day you might think, though in fact it was early in the day.

Floating upstairs I found her double bed of golden pine with its slatted headboard, the white linen all rumpled and unmade. I touched things and peered inside cupboards, quite enjoying the ghostly feeling.

Down again. My husband was in her kitchen, making pastry and using too much flour, likely result, dry and falling apart. He greeted me with Oh.

I have nothing to say to you, I thought of replying, but opted instead for where are the kids?

Lounge, he flourily pointed.

My children were playing with gadgets and watching TV. The rabbit observed me sideways from its place on the sofa.

Darlings! I made a little speech, informing them: you don't belong here, you live next door. Put down your gadgets, I said (they didn't) and follow me (they did).

Having warned them to mind the gap, I stood a right-eous sentry as they jumped across. One child, two child, three child, no rabbit. I slammed the door. The kids ran up and downstairs, laughing and shouting about the colour of the bathroom. Meanwhile my hand stayed stuck to the door handle as pain lit through me and plunged down the gap to earth itself below floorboard level. Its cause (why pretend otherwise) the rabbit's absence. My buddy, my betrayer.

Night. I slept dreamlessly but woke to a midnight vision, shining at the foot of my bed. The rabbit! It addressed me in a high and trembling voice: to the last, I did my duty as your loyal friend. And when I say the last, let me clarify – keen to follow you home as requested, I hopped off the sofa, landed clumsily, broke a leg and died in lonely agony. You never checked to see if I was OK…

Oh rabbit, I'm so sorry. I assumed –

I know. But you wronged me.

Well at least let me venerate your memory by giving you a proper funeral. All the honours! I'll demand they hand over your little furry corpse, whatever its current condition. If she threw it in the trash, I'll kill her!

The spirit rabbit's nose twitched. Got to be going… It shuffled to the bed's edge. Wait, aren't ghosts supposed to just fade away?

I grabbed it in mid leap. It kicked and struggled in my arms, trying to bite me as I rushed downstairs with it, my former guide and adviser, now prisoner/hostage. And me furiously transfigured, a hunting owl, a seething serpent…

Depositing my false friend in an armchair – sit here, I told it, and don't you dare move!

The door in the wall was shut, no nose-through gap, but clue: a pile of child-related stuff had been shoved back, doubtless plus rabbit. Time for an honest convo re. actual events in their true sequence. I turned: but although still present, a quivering rabbit-on-a-cushion, my rabbit had essentially gone, bolted into its old animal self.

Exchange of stolid stares: rabbit–woman and vice versa. Woman outwitted, rabbit incommunicado. Whoosh, anger deflated. I pulled a throw off the sofa, wrapped it round me and went to fill the kettle for a cuppa.

Aggrieved injury had bolstered my resolve, but in the absence of upset I started to regret things. She's behaved better than me, I thought – showing dignity, observing boundaries. She never entered my house uninvited.

Next thought: I was never a particularly good wife and mother. Ah well.

I fished the teabag out of my mug and dumped it on the work surface, heedless of pool and stain. How pleasant it felt to be unmarried, or at least on marital hiatus. What a relief actually.

Just then, as though contrarily conjured by my first sniff of the wild and weedy fields of freedom, he reappeared. In our house, not hers. Bugger.

It's not working out, he said. Please can I come home? Barefoot and shivering in paisley pyjamas, strange to me and kind of touching in their bad taste. Not her choice, surely. The kitchen looks different, have you painted it?

Nothing's changed, I said into his pyjama-clad chest. You only think it has. This sounded deeper and more forgiving than I'd intended. Memory cheats your perception, I thought of adding but didn't as his arms tightened around me and I breathed in his smell, noting she uses a different detergent. It's always been umber walls, maple cupboards.

He proposed reaffirming our commitment. Did I really want this, I wondered briefly. A kiss sealed the deal. Then having thrown my teabag in the bin, he took a cloth and wiped the formica. He uttered not a word of reproach. I knew it wouldn't be long, though.

We've since had many a spat. Last night he challenged me, did you ever wonder why we all left: your husband, your children, even the rabbit?

Irrelevant, Captain, because at the end of the day / in the middle of the night I got them all back again. Rabbit, kids, husband.

I wonder if she's miserable now, I suspect not. I imagine she must be greatly relieved, to be alone again.

Sometimes I trace with my fingertips the doorway's outline, it's still there, although the plasterer covered it over.

Meanwhile the rabbit has become extremely patronising. Yesterday as I was cleaning out its hutch, while it made a lettuce leaf steadily vanish – I don't know how it manages to talk and eat at the same time – it told me, you went back on your own best instincts. Weak, but understandable. A heroic life of lonely sacrifice isn't for everyone, I quite see that.

Passive Youth

They slump in chairs and on sofas, or lie on the carpet and we have to step over them. Their dishes and cutlery pile by the kitchen sink; we spend a good part of each day washing up. Trying to find love for them in our hearts, or any non-negative emotion, we greet them with cheerful politeness. In response we get silence, the occasional grunt.

Their rooms are a mess. We don't tidy up for fear of offending them, but every now and then we collect their dirty clothes to put in the washing machine and hang on the line. We steel ourselves to clean their toilet, using powerful chemicals. In the shower we find a strange orange mould, never previously encountered. Coming downstairs again, we groan and hold our hands to our backs. We have arthritis, fibromyalgia. They don't sympathise, never ask us how we are.

They seem to have no serious thought of leaving. We've shown them estate agents' details, places for rent, but they're not interested. Girlfriends come and go, young women with lives of their own, jobs, flats. At first they seem happy, then puzzled and finally annoyed. Voices are raised, our front door is slammed, cars drive away.

We suspect they're waiting us out – hoping eventually to inherit the house, plus our savings accounts, so they'll never have to go anywhere, do anything, take any sort of initiative. But we don't resent this, it's natural. We worry about how they'll cope, after we're gone.

Observing Lucy

At first to survive and then to do well in life, it is necessary often to stifle impulse; to set up in nature's place *une caractère*; to deny the past. So the holy nun and the successful businesswoman have much in common. And while charity is enjoined upon us, our generosity may have unforeseen consequences. As in the case of Mlle Lucy.

One night there came a knock on the *porte-cochère* of my *Pensionnat des Demoiselles* in the Rue Fossette. A young woman, a foreigner and a stranger, stood there in the rain, soaked through and pale with exhaustion. Failing to recognise in her an agent of the Evil One, I let her in. That was my very great mistake.

For nursery-governesses, I choose always *les Anglaises*. Mlle Lucy suited the post. However, in braiding and arranging my hair she proved clumsy. At 41, I still had plentiful bright auburn hair and I took some pride over its appearance. My figure was somewhat stout but I dressed myself well, in silks of dark colours. Mlle Lucy's typical attire was a muted grey and her complexion lacked freshness; she was always neat, however.

I decided to try her as a teacher and was surprised by

her courage in dealing with the girls. The little mouse became a warrior. Having introduced her to the class, I left; through a spyhole I watched as she tore in two the composition of Mlle de Melcy, as she caught Mlle Dolores off balance and pushed her into a cupboard. *C'est bien*, I told myself. *Ça ira.*

My husband, who has skill in physiognomy, expressed doubts. In her face he perceived both good and evil. One of these would in time come to the fore and seize power. But which? "Impossible to judge. Above all," he continued, "she is lonely and starved of affection. But dangerous in that respect. Like a wild animal seeking its prey."

"Comme Zélie St Pierre?"

"Mais non, pas la même chose." And having then adjusted his tasselled nightcap on his close-clipped skull, Paul rolled away from me and commenced to snore. Perhaps I sighed a little – for I too was a woman in need of affection – yet I admonished myself, Modeste, what do you expect? Our marital life is sufficient. He has given you three healthy children.

In the succeeding days and months, Mlle Lucy compelled my attention. I became in a way fascinated by her. A nature so very different from my own; yet in our mutual watchfulness and reserve, perhaps more similar than she imagined. Loving to be alone, at sunset or the hour of *salut* she would often slip away into the garden. She favoured in particular a secluded and shadowy walk, *l'allée défendue*, where she herself had cleaned a bench of mould and dirt. Here she – this good daughter of the English Church – gazed upon the moon and worshipped her.

One little incident served to amuse me. Not long after Mlle Lucy had joined my teaching staff, Zélie St Pierre naturally attempted to seduce her. She took Lucy's hand and stroked her arm, half-rose and would have pressed her lips – but no, Mlle Lucy started back in horror! Then came many good French words, for by this time *l'Anglaise* had mastered *notre langue* to perfection. How she castigated La St Pierre, decrying her as a serpent, Lucifer in female form! I laughed behind my spyhole. Such a drama, to proceed from an event in itself so paltry.

That year on my birthday morning, the sun rose hot and unclouded. As is customary, all the doors and windows were set open. The *coiffeur* arrived at nine and wrought his magic on girls and teachers; the *habillement* then took three hours. Passing Mlle Lucy on the stairs, I nodded approval of her quiet style. I too was dressed *convenablement*, in dove-coloured silk. My only ornament was a large gold brooch set with rubies, a present from my husband.

I was in the kitchen with Goton, checking her preparations for the gala tea – the baker had just then supplied eight trays of mixed patisseries – when Paul came in. "Quel désastre! Louise Vanderkelkov has fallen ill. No other girl will accept her role in the play, since it is that of a man. And there is hardly any time left..."

"Ask Mlle Lucy to play the part," I said.

"Quoi? Cette Prude Anglaise!"

"She will do it, if you ask." He rushed off. I laughed to myself, imagining the quandary of Mlle Lucy. Although no doubt horrified at the thought of appearing on stage, *surtout* as a masculine character, she would be unable to resist the challenge. I began to know something of her nature.

The hours passed quickly, all gay and glad. Presented with a case of silver plate, I acted great surprise. Then all the girls dispersed into the garden, where the collation was laid out on trestle tables. My husband waved a key in my face triumphantly: he had locked Mlle Lucy in the attic to learn her lines! With my own hands I assembled a plate of food, at my urging he took it up to her.

As day glided into evening, the time for the vaudeville drew near. A stage had been set up on the long room, concealed by a green curtain; a row of footlights waited to blaze. Paul hurried Mlle Lucy down from her garret and shoved her onstage. Before she could take fright and bolt, the curtain shrivelled to the ceiling. *Et voilà!* The audience politely clapped, but also I heard some tittering. Without laying her dress aside, Mlle Lucy had added trousers, to peculiar effect. Fortunately she was not to play the hero, but a man of no worth, a figure of fun. She and the pretty Mlle Fanshawe began their scene of idle courtship well enough. But then a note of earnest crept in. These two girls in effect tore up the script, instead they played true lovers. And to a marvel! The audience was charmed and entertained.

As for me, I became as stone. A creature that lurked deep in my bowels, the quick of my nature, stirred and was brought alive in response to *l'Anglaise,* or to this character performed by her. I felt Zélie St Pierre's eyes upon me. At the end of the play I clapped without enthusiasm, then arranged my skirts and led the way to the ballroom.

My husband and Mlle Fanshawe began the dancing. Indeed all the male dancing partners were *pères de famille.* Some *jeune gens,* brothers and cousins of the girls, had been admitted as spectators, but these I herded behind a rope in the furthest corner of the *carré.* For the rest of the evening I patrolled them, cheerful and bustling, and also concealed any sign of my discomposure. In both endeavours I succeeded well.

Ah Lucy, what secret groans and tears you have cost me! My enemy, feared even to the point of hatred... The duty of surveillance became for me almost a compulsion. I see myself now in the gathering dusk, in my shawl, wrapping-gown and slippers, investigating her workbox and the locked drawers beneath. Here are five letters, tied with a blue ribbon, the broken seal impressed with the initials J.G.B. I extract the heavy vellum pages from their envelopes and read them each in turn. A spider runs across the floor. From beginning to end I see no word of love, only at most a gentle friendship. But who can tell? *Les Anglais* do not understand the first thing about passion.

My manner towards her was kind, even prudently affectionate. For instance, I warned her not to study too much, lest the blood should go to her head. I patted her and called her *ma chère amie*. Modeste, I told myself, you could have been a great actress.

While reading her letters in the attic, Mlle Lucy had a hysterical collapse and afterwards claimed to have seen the ghost of a nun. This nonsense irritated me. But again I was kind.

Meanwhile, I took steps to conquer my hidden and shameful desire, until at last I was ready to bid it a final farewell. I remembered a tale from *Les Mille et Une Nuits,* a volume bound in calfskin that my mother had long ago sold to the dealers, along with the rest of my father's library. A sultan chose a young and innocent girl to be one of his harem. Brought up in strict seclusion, she had never before laid eyes upon a man. Then one day, happening to glance down from a turret, she noticed a youth at work in the palace gardens. "How beautiful he is!" she exclaimed. With regret, the sultan gave orders for this girl and the so-admired young man to be buried alive together in a large box under a spreading tree. He then reclined upon a bench placed on the same spot, and meditated upon Love. Of course, the unfortunate couple were interred too deep for their cries to reach and disturb him.

With this salutary tale in mind, and resolved to conquer my own disposition, I searched for and found an old trinket box, no longer of any use to me. In this I placed the ashes of a blank sheet of paper. After dinner, when the moon had risen, I shawled myself and stole into the garden. Mlle Lucy was at this time absent from La Rue Fossette, so I entered *l'allée défendue* without fear. Having cleared away ivy from around the roots of an ancient pear tree, I thrust my box into a deep hollow. Then I sat on Lucy's bench and breathed deeply of the good night air. I felt, I will not say peaceful, but reconciled to myself.

As the moon emerged from clouds and shone down, a shrouded figure approached. She paused about three yards away and we regarded each other. It was the ghostly nun described to me by Mlle Lucy. Robed and veiled – yes, exactly. But in stature, short. Mlle Lucy's terrified recollection had added at least ten inches to her height.

"Who are you?" I demanded. She stood mute. Refusing to be intimidated, I pounced upon her and tore off her veil. She wore a moustache! In fact she was Colonel Alfred de Hamal, one of Mlle Fanshawe's many suitors. They had no doubt made an assignation to meet here. With a cry of rage, I grabbed a spade I had brought with me from the tool shed and raised it high. De Hamal squeaked in terror and fled, a sight most amusing.

This incident proved what I already knew well, that watchfulness and caution are at all times necessary. To *la surveillance* I clung when the ground beneath my feet seemed to melt away. I trusted nobody, only my husband, on whose discretion I relied entirely. His absences at first did not alarm me, for being devout, he often stays at a retreat centre in the lower town. However, one fine day, in early spring, as I crossed the lawn to the *berceau*, where he was digging the soil and putting in bulbs, I overheard voices, his and that of Mlle Lucy. I crept behind a tree and listened. His manner towards Lucy was gentle, tender. He described himself to her as poor, burdened and lonely. He asked her to be his little sister.

That night I asked him why he had never spoken in such a way to me, his wife? "I was attempting to console her," he replied. "She is weak, you are strong. You do not need my pity."

In fact Mlle Lucy is strong as a python, despite her hysterics. But no use to argue, since he had fallen in love with her. I resolved henceforth to keep a close eye on them and to interpose myself at every opportunity. If I could not up-root their love, at least I could snip its leaves and deprive it of light and air.

I enlisted the help of Père Silas, Paul's confessor and good friend, a Jesuit with the nose for sin of a bloodhound. Yet still they evaded our scrutiny. At length, with some reluctance, I terminated Mlle Lucy's employment. "You must leave," I told her. "The situation has become unten-able."

Of course, she spat insults at me – "dog in the manger" being among the most mysterious. Then she went upstairs to pack her things. Having ascertained the next sailing times of vessels to England, and intending to hand her a note of these through the door, I again found her and Paul whispering together.

Quite unabashed he turned on me, "Sortez d'ici!"

I stood my ground and threatened to send for Père Si-las. But he persisted: "Laissez-moi!" Then his face became suffused with rage. He took a few quick steps towards me and slapped me, hard. I whirled from the room; not before I had seen Mlle Lucy smile.

L'Anglaise therefore did not immediately leave Villette, as I had desired her to. Instead, aided by my husband – who gave her money that was mine alone! – she set up a rival teaching establishment.

In retrospect, their affair was so predictable. *Bien enten-du*, they shared a certain intensity of spirit. No other men were at that time available to her. And the English lack morals. She took him without a qualm and became his mistress. Eventually he tired of his new plaything, his doll in her doll's house, and he returned to me. He admits that he was foolish, but maintains they never slept together.

Mlle Lucy has since written a novel, I am informed – a strange confection of lies and wishful imaginings, based upon her time at La Rue Fossette. Now I ask you, the reader: if my husband slapped me only lightly, why was my face so bruised that I must hide myself away in my *chambre* for days and have meals brought up to me by Goton? If he was not in fact my husband, how did I obtain my three children – were they conceived through a miracle, by an angel's visit from heaven? And if at last he died tragically in a shipwreck, is it then a ghost who sleeps in my bed?

The Poetry Course

Given the amount of time Brantley had been down the hole, it was amazing his single, lidless eye could still focus. Well, it wasn't really a hole. Once you got through the entrance tunnel it was more of a lair. With big rooms, some carpeted and furnished, others never used. A suitable residence for the last of the dragons, which Brantley sort of was, although after centuries of inbreeding he didn't look much like a dragon, more (but still not very) like a human being.

It was home, but gloomy. To save electricity, Brantley kept the lights and the fridge switched off. His computer was powered by wind energy – a small turbine in the overgrown garden, only just visible to passers-by.

Bradley was waiting to hear from the Arval Foundation. He'd applied in January for a place on a course in Advanced Poetry and now it was June, only a month till the course. Perhaps he should just assume his application had been successful. He'd sent ten pages of his epic poem about Griffin Drake, his uncle, and a writing history of twenty pages, describing his own years of struggle, the creative blocks, the rejections by publishers. He'd considered editing it down, but had decided not to.

Two things in particular were now worrying Brantley: (1) he snored, as do all dragons, and he might have to share a room, according to the brochure; (2) the course tutors were Osmund Scarlet and Nina Horner. Brantley might say Oswald by mistake and then Osmund might be offended. Well, at least Nina was an easy name to remember. She wrote sonnets and villanelles, about canaries, bats and nightingales. Brantley preferred runic verse, if he was honest.

But an Arval course! People's lives were transformed by going on Arval courses. The tutors recommended their work to agents. They became part of the literary world. And so might he, why not? A dragon writing dragonlit. Splendid for blurbs.

Thinking that the post must have come by now, Brantley put on a wide-brimmed hat with a gauze veil, to protect his eye from insects and specks of dirt, and went to check the box.

It was terribly bright outside.

The box was empty. No confirmation letter from Arval. No books from Boudicca.co.uk. Nothing.

Brantley felt depressed and lonely. Deciding on impulse to ring the Arval centre, he collected the brochure from his bedside table. Then with all the details to paw, he tapped in the number.

"Excuse me, I'm very sorry to bother you, but..."

The calm administrator asked his name and said she would look at the database. Seconds later: "No, you're not on the course," she said. "You haven't been chosen. But you're on the reserve list."

"Thank you very much," said Brantley, and put down the phone. He sat stunned. Then a tear fell from his eye.

Not chosen. Reserve list, what did that mean? Hanging around waiting and being humbly available, in case someone dropped out.

The phone rang. But it wasn't the administrator ringing to say she'd made a mistake. It was Aunt Julia.

"Hello," sobbed Brantley. "Yes, very well thank you, Aunt Julia. How are you?"

Aunt Julia was only a dragon by marriage – she'd been Uncle Griffin's eighteenth and last wife. He'd left her a very nice lair, fully furnished and heaped with jewels. Brantley didn't grudge her one single garnet or bit of rose quartz. Uncle Griffin couldn't have been easy to live with: he'd hatched in a bad temper, which hadn't improved over the next thousand years or so. He'd also been something of a Bluebeard. One room still remained locked, its key hanging in the kitchen cupboard. Aunt Julia's incurious nature, plus her philosophy of 'Let sleeping or possibly dead dragons lie,' had promoted household harmony during Uncle Griffin's lifetime, while enabling her to survive into widowhood.

"Brantley, what's wrong? Is it that back incisor?"

"No, but. Well. Oh, Aunt Julia..." It all came pouring out.

"Who are these people?" she boomed. "I've never heard of them." Aunt Julia didn't read poetry, so this wasn't really surprising, but it made him feel slightly better.

"Look here, Brantley. They obviously realised they couldn't teach you anything. Because you're a much more Advanced Poet than they are. You're in a higher league altogether."

"I don't think so, Aunt Julia." Sniff. "But thank you."

"Griffin always used to say how good you were. And he ran a flying school!"

Brantley slept well that night and woke resolved. He emailed the Arval Centre to let them know his decision and asked them to send back his deposit cheque.

Then he sat on a tree stump in the garden, watching the seeds blowing down from the wych elm in their little round paper cases. Remembering a riddle popular in the

Drake family: I have a single, lidless eye. Who am I?

London, the riddle-solver might say. Or a lighthouse. Those were both good answers.

The postman came by, whistling. "Morning, Mr Drake." Brantley said hello. He watched the seeds, the clouds, a beetle in the grass. His mind went still and then he thought of a new verse for his epic poem. It just came to him, without any effort, like a flower unfolding its petals in the light.

Gone to War

She thought he was playing a friendly cricket match on the village green, but he'd got his call-up papers. While doing the washing up she heard muffled explosions and thought they're probably taking down that block of flats, an eyesore, good riddance. She looked at her hands, all wrinkled from the soapy water, and thought I must get some gloves. When she turned round from the sink there he was, dirty and bloody. The words you've been gone a long time died or vapourised in her mouth. Well I'm back, he said. Haven't you got a kiss?

A Game of Queens

Elizabeth was serious, focused, determined. She conducted her love affairs discreetly and used social media for work purposes only. Though she enjoyed sex, she also believed in planning ahead. After all, she was nearly thirty.

"But why him?" a friend challenged her across a white tablecloth in a Greek restaurant.

Elizabeth shrugged. "Why any him?"

"Well, exactly. I always thought if you ever did get married…"

Elizabeth rearranged the condiments. "I'm quite old-fashioned. And he's safe, a safe bet. I've already decided what I want." She passed the menu. "We're going to visit his parents this weekend. They still live in the house where he grew up."

"Gosh, parents."

"Yes, parents. His."

"Sorry, I'm still just gobsmacked."

Elizabeth and Philip dealt with work emails on the train, occasionally looking up to exchange smiles. "I've told Mom and Pop about us. They're delighted," he'd mentioned earlier that week at the photocopier.

"Mom and Pop?"

"Family joke."

"Do you have lots of family jokes?"

"A fair few. But don't worry, you'll love us."

Miles and miles of dull countryside. "Shall we get a taxi from the station?"

"No need. Mater will pick us up in the Fiat Punto." He phoned his mother and lied, winking: "We've just passed Ockham."

Station forecourt. A woman in shape-concealing layers flourished a dark cloth and cried "Introduce us!"

"Mimsy-Mumsy, this is Elizabeth. Liz, Mamacita."

Discoloured teeth. A grasp that left fingertip-sized bruises on Elizabeth's arm. "In this pestery outsider time, what shall we call you?"

Elizabeth: "I don't mind, anything…."

"Just his girlfriend, then. Until you're bound inseparable unto the clayey grave – my word, your plentiful blonde hair will make excellent nests for mice. You go in the back, Phil." Mrs Walker gave her wing mirrors a final polish and opened the front passenger door for Elizabeth. "Hop aboard; don't be nervous. Among other safety features, automatic locks prevent escape or suicide."

"Joke," said Philip. "Ha!"

Mrs Walker pointed out the amenities as they sped past. "Crap post office … Co-op, limited stock and a superfluity of busybodies … health centre, avoid avoid. War memorial, cemetery."

The car stopped outside a 1930s house in a modern cul-de-sac. "We used to be semi-detached; our other half got knocked down. The less said, the fewer restless spirits."

It was very quiet in the cul-de-sac.

Indoors, having told Philip to "pop up and visit Leo. And take the bags with you," Mrs Walker resumed her commentary. Of three reception rooms: "Seldom used,

they just create dust, languishing in stasis." The
were decorated and furnished in neutral shades,
some feature wallpaper and stripped pine floorboard

"It's like the Tardis," Elizabeth felt duty bound to say.
Mrs Walker gave no sign of having heard her. Instead she
led the way along a corridor that changed at one point
into a tunnel carved through rock. Flaring torches in cer-
emonial procession: Mrs Walker an ancient regal figure,
Elizabeth her young successor. Ahead, a fire-lit cave; drum
beats...

"Watch out, there's a little step down," Mrs Walker said
over her shoulder. She introduced the kitchen: "Our family room." Someone long and pale lay outstretched on a
tattered sofa: "My husband, Phil's pa. Best to ignore him.
Reads all the time. A man."

Philip's father, who looked almost identical to Philip,
hefted his book like a caber before placing it on the floor.
"Early retirement on medical grounds. Excellent pension,
got out just in time. Financial mainstay, though from the
way she talks about me..."

Offered tea and invited to sit down, Elizabeth glanced
about her. The kitchen cupboards were painted wartime
green; patterned lino and hand-hooked rugs suggested
old-fashioned homeliness, in a museum-like way.

Mrs Walker addressed her husband, quietly but audi-
bly: "What do you think?"

"Splendid, splendid. An absolute bobby-dazzler. So
you work with Phil?" Mr Walker segued fluently into a
description of his own former co-workers and managers,
their resistance to logical argument, his struggle to enforce
a minor point of procedure...

Mrs Walker interrupted: "Drunk your tea? Then let's
go upstairs."

The corridor was just a corridor, Elizabeth noted. Stairs
swirled up to a broad, flowery-carpeted landing.

A stencilled notice on a door warned: DON'T come in.

Or you will DIE.

Mrs Walker opened the door and went in. "Lenore, this is Elizabeth. Try to be nice to her, she's your brother's… remember what we talked about."

A child of nine or ten glowered at them from a magenta bedspread. Her dark hair was pulled back, then rioted in a complication of plaits.

"Hello" Elizabeth said.

"Hello."

"What a lovely room."

"Pink for a girl's bedroom. I don't like it myself and nor does she, but it's the façade. Are you convinced?" Mrs Walker asked Elizabeth. "No, just polite and well-mannered. But you'll soon be family, you're safe enough."

Safe, safe – the word rang tinnily off-key in Elizabeth's mind. Safe from her own past self maybe. That clearly wasn't what Mrs Walker meant, though. What did Mrs Walker mean?

And where was Philip?

"I've put you and Phil in the guest bedroom." Mrs Walker said as they re-crossed the landing. "Overlooking the garden and concealed from scrutiny. I'm sure you value your privacy, I do mine."

The room was dingy and furnished with bunk beds. "There!" – Mrs Walker proudly pointed. "I suggest you take the lower one. Phil's always falling out of bed, knocks himself unconscious, it's quite a sport to him."

"Right, thank you. Lovely. By the way, where is Philip? I thought he might be…"

Beckoning, Mrs Walker strode back to Lenore's room and commanded a bank of soft toys by the window to "Reveal yourself!" She added: "Don't glare at me, Leo. He's not your plaything."

Fists shot out, then arms lifted and threw off the cuddly camouflage. "Joke!" said Philip. "Ha! Ha!"

Elizabeth, feeling in need of some brief contact with the

outside world: "I wonder if I can get a signal here?"

"A signal." Mrs Walker looked at Philip. He mimed putting up the aerial of a walkie-talkie. "Oh! No, I don't think we have a signal. But you're welcome to search around, perhaps in the garden."

Elizabeth had glimpsed the garden from the window of the bunk bed room. A rectangular lawn surrounded by dark pines and brilliant green false cypresses, creating the effect of a skewed chessboard…

Clutching her shoulder bag, she ran downstairs and let herself out of the front door. "Just leave it on the latch!" Mrs Walker shouted.

The door fitted snugly back into its arched frame. Still no sign of life in the cul-de-sac, apart from some large birds sitting on chimney pots.

Elizabeth walked along near-identical suburban roads: Anubis Avenue, Bludfield Crescent, Crops Circle, High Hornets, Little Middle Way. The latticed steel bridge of the railway station came into view between two houses. She rummaged in her bag, found her purse.

Meanwhile, back at the house, Philip was throwing himself downstairs. Repeatedly, each time from higher up. Mrs Walker stepped over his body on her way to the kitchen.

The Walker family's Phil and the Philip she'd known in London seemed like two different people to Elizabeth. Hard to judge though, on such short acquaintance. I don't love him, she thought, I'm only quite fond of him.

"Quite fond has lasted me decades" – Mrs Walker spoke from a privet hedge. "Supper will be ready in less than an hour," she leafily added. "I've done all the food preparation and set the table. You'll be sitting opposite me."

Ignoring the hedge, Elizabeth adjusted the strap of her bag. I'm not a coward, she thought, whatever else I may be.

The door was still on the latch and Philip in the guest

bedroom, changing.

"Should I change too?" she asked.

"Nah."

"You've got bruises…"

He craned his head. "Slipped and bashed myself in the shower."

"And on your arms and legs."

"So there are. Weird." He donned a clean white shirt, trousers and a dinner jacket. "Ready to go down?"

Mrs Walker, regal in a sparkly floor-sweeper and holding a tea towel, emerged from the little back kitchen to inform Elizabeth graciously: "No obligation. Whatever we wear betrays our nakedness. Sit, sit!" She herded them all to the table. Elizabeth saw with relief that Lenore and Mr Walker were still casually dressed.

Blue ceramic dishes were placed in front of her. "Dolmades, oh wow! Lamb souvlaki!"

"It's fresh-caught field lamb," said Mrs Walker. "We live so near the countryside, I'd be ashamed to buy a packaged animal."

"Did Philip tell you I love Greek food?" Elizabeth served herself and tried to pass the dishes round, but the others were already eating a traditional English meal. "Saturday, chops," Mr Walker informed her.

"I think I just knew," said Mrs Walker.

Despite her foreknowledge of Elizabeth's tastes, there was no red wine; they drank water poured from a jug. Lenore picked up her chop by the bone and transferred it to her mother's plate, in what seemed to be an established ritual.

'Pudding' was baklava for Elizabeth – "Made from scratch," said Mrs Walker. "Scratch being the operative word." – while the family had jam tart and custard. Lenore was then permitted to 'get down'.

They drank coffee in one of the reception rooms. Like a stage set, thought Elizabeth. "I have a proposal to make:

let's form a book club!" Mrs Walker handed round copies of a small book with a red cloth cover. "It's about a shark."

"A whale," corrected Mr Walker. "But there are sharks in it."

They sat reading in silence. Mrs Walker sighed at intervals. The men held their books up close to their faces.

Elizabeth, rousing herself from sleep: "I think I'll take a quick walk around the garden..."

"You can't get through those doors, they're painted shut."

Elizabeth grasped a slim brass oval and turned it. The patio doors creaked open, disproving Mrs Walker's assertion, and she hurried along a gleaming metallic path in the moonlight. Giant knights, bishops and rooks cast long shadows on the chequered lawn. Beyond the trees she discovered more garden: tangled shrubbery and moss-slimed paving stones, a bell hanging on a rope over a picket gate. A bench, on which sat Mrs Walker. "Don't mind me dear, I'm just moonlighting. Up there is an owl, hunting mice. To woo!"

Elizabeth tried to speak, but could only utter moaning vowels. To woo! – the owl swooped down. She jolted awake. Philip's parents were smiling fondly at her. The red cloth books sat in a neat pile on the coffee table.

"Cocoa?" said Mrs Walker.

"No thanks."

"Good night then, dear. Sweet dreams."

Philip was already snoring in the top bunk. Half-way along the corridor to the bathroom, Mrs Walker brandished a frayed toothbrush.

Elizabeth held up her own electric model. "I'm OK, thanks."

"Oh! But can you get a signal?"

"It doesn't need a signal."

"How clever."

Lying in bed, it occurred to Elizabeth her toothbrush

might run out of power. In which case she'd just use it like an ordinary one. Drawn swords, she thought.

The door opened, admitting a line of light. Rustles and creaks. Somebody else was in the room. "Hello?"

Lenore sat down, trapping Elizabeth's legs under the duvet. "I can't sleep." She reached out to touch Elizabeth's face. "Now I'm sixteen, I just want to get started. Help me..."

"Sixteen? I don't think that can be true."

"A lot of true things exist beyond human perception," said Lenore, sharp amid clouds of hair. "And at night."

Elizabeth, too tired to argue: "I'm your mother's guest." Lenore made an impatient clicking noise and left.

Women were filling vases and decorating pew ends, while Bridge Over Troubled Water played on a loop. Mrs Walker strode up the aisle: "This way..." One of the flower arrangers upset her bucket and screamed a profanity.

Tapestry cushions below the altar rail depicted lively scenes. Mrs Walker sank down, pulling at Elizabeth. "I'm not religious myself, at least not in any modern sense. But try it now." Elizabeth, kneeling too, switched on her phone and got a signal.

"Marry in an old church, then in times of trial – sod's law – you can call upon ancient forces. By the bye, will you change your name?"

"No."

"But the other thing?"

"I haven't decided."

"It's so important to us. Children optional." Elizabeth got up abruptly. Mrs Walker accompanied her at a brisk pace back down the aisle and through a goggle of flower arrangers.

They walked out of the church together, Mrs Walker humming and la-la-ing Simon & Garfunkel. Leonore showered them with confetti, then ran off laughing and jumping over graves. Not sixteen, Elizabeth thought.

"I had a terrible time giving birth to Phil," Mrs Walker confided. "Which may explain it. Or it could be hereditary. He'll irritate you, of course." She wafted a ringed hand, then bent to pick up a mauve paper bone and a pink skull: "Funeral confetti! Leo's like you, very clever and original. She just slithered out of me."

They drove home along a straight road edged by wood and fields. "Sometimes I think the family is a laughable construction. But without it we're ghosts or monsters."

"Scary."

"Yes, we are."

Insects began to hit the windscreen. Mrs Walker turned on the wipers, which smeared red. "Oh not again." Crossly she pulled into a layby and searched in the glove compartment. Armed with a cloth and a bottle of 'squirty stuff' she attacked the blood and bugs, and polished the glass to a shine.

Back on the road: "Such a pity you can't stay a bit longer. I don't suppose there's any chance – no. But we could chat on the telephone, perhaps. Or even..." Her eyes like a hunting owl. In my dreams, Elizabeth thought.

Words hopped from her lips: "Allow me sovereignty over my own domain." Aargh, Walker-speak! "Sorry, I meant..."

"Point taken," said Mrs Walker. "You remind me so much of myself as a young woman."

Platform 2, far end. A black-and-white notice warned Elizabeth: DON'T go beyond this point. Or you will DIE.

The tracks, the wooded embankment...

Philip was waiting vacantly by the ticket office, next to his mother. Upon Elizabeth's return he started up again: "Hello, old girl!"

"The place beyond," said Mrs Walker. "So good for wildlife, now they've stopped hacking back the vegetation."

In slid the train and they boarded. Mrs Walker tearfully waved her insect-coated cloth. "Lovely time... birds of beak and claw... fly back soon!"

Another glimpse: Mrs Walker ignoring the exit, striding off along the platform. Where's she going, Elizabeth wondered.

Philip smiled at her over his laptop lid as the train sped them city-wards. "Bit overpowering? She can be."

"Not in the least," said Elizabeth. "We're more similar than otherwise."

Looking Out

Opening the kitchen door on her hands and knees in the dewy early morning, Lizzie smelled honeysuckle, then somewhat painfully adjusting her position to peer around the door frame, she saw a couple of pale yellow flowers perched on a tendril that had wound itself over the fence from next door, also she noticed how from this low place the garden looked mysterious, winding into an unknown future beyond the purple clematis on the shed, and remembering her tiny walnut tree, grown from a nut, she thought she would go out later—the step would be the hardest bit—and turn the pot around, to help it grow straight.

Acknowledgements

Stories from this collection have been read aloud at, or featured in: Polari at the mac birmingham, thank you to Polari curator and host Paul Burston ('Jingaling a-Bobbin, Like Apples in a Barrel'); the S@veAs Writers 'Writing the City' awards event, thank you to competition judge Maria C. McCarthy of Cultured Llama and chairman/host Luigi Marchini ('Broken Thing'); and a festival tent in Saskatoon, thank you to competition judge Yann Martel ('Watery').

Many thanks also to the publishers and editors of: *Spontaneity* ('The Leaf that Wouldn't Fall'); *Necrologue, the Diva Book of the Dead and the Undead,* ed. Helen Sandler, Diva Books ('There Was an Old Woman'); *Extinguished & Extinct – An Anthology of Things That No Longer Exist*, ed. John McCarthy, Twelve Winters Press ('Cleaner'); *Short Fiction* 1 and 7, ed. Anthony Caleshu, University of Plymouth Press ('It Was' and 'In the Wild Wood'); *Origins*, Creative Industries Trafford ('Bluebeard's Daughter'); *Litro* ('The Estate'), *The London Magazine* online ('The Golden Hour'); *The Irish Literary Review* ('Had a Heart'); *Matchbook Stories: Issue Four*, Book Ex Machina ('My Lion'); *Silver Apples Magazine* ('Married to a Carrot'); *Upshots and Other Stories*, Spread the Word and Kingston University Press ('The Moustache Maker's Daughter'); *Stories for Homes*, ed. Sally Swingewood and Debi Alper ('Babylon'); *L Is For*, ed. Kiki Archer, Jayne Fereday and Angela Peach ('In Bed with Miss Lucas'); *Hark* ('The Society of Lost Souls'); *The Moth*, Issue 13 ('A Bit of Tragedy'); *Poems for a Liminal Age*, ed. Mandy Pannett, SPM Publications ('Stepmother', 'Seagull', 'Mourning Angel' and 'Catching Fire'); *Mslexia*, guest editors Michelle Roberts and Julia Darling ('Sister Joy and the Spider' and 'Small Tall'); *New Writing 13*, ed. Ali Smith and Toby Litt, Picador with the British Council and Arts Council England ('Teeth and Hair'); *RiverLit* ('Marriage Counselling'); *Cactus Heart* ('The People Before Me'); *The Day of the Dead and Other Stories*, Black Pear Press ('Blackbird'); *The Refugees Welcome Anthology* ('I Should Go Back to the Dance Class'); 22 Tiny Tales, Flash Frontier and National Flash Fiction Day NZ ('Be Wise'); *Inside These Tangles, Beauty Lies,* Retreat West ('Oxygen for a Minotaur'); *Full Moon & Foxglove: An Anthology of Witches & Witchcraft*, ed. Kate Garrett, Three Drops Press ('The Hairs on my Chinny-chin-chin'); The Linnet's Wings ('Passive Youth'); Defenestration ('The Poetry Course'); and Camroc Press Review ('Looking Out').

Cultured Llama Publishing
Poems | Stories | Curious Things

Cultured Llama was born in a converted stable. This creature of humble birth drank greedily from the creative source of the poets, writers, artists and musicians that visited, and soon the llama fulfilled the destiny of its given name.

Cultured Llama aspires to quality from the first creative thought through to the finished product.

www.culturedllama.co.uk

Also published by Cultured Llama

Poetry

strange fruits by Maria C. McCarthy
Paperback; 72pp; 203×127mm; 978-0-9568921-0-2; July 2011

A Radiance by Bethany W. Pope
Paperback; 70pp; 203×127mm; 978-0-9568921-3-3; June 2012

The Strangest Thankyou by Richard Thomas
Paperback; 98pp; 203×127mm; 978-0-9568921-5-7; November 2012

The Night My Sister Went to Hollywood by Hilda Sheehan
Paperback; 82pp; 203×127mm; 978-0-9568921-8-8; March 2013

Notes from a Bright Field by Rose Cook
Paperback; 104pp; 203×127mm; 978-0-9568921-9-5; July 2013

Sounds of the Real World by Gordon Meade
Paperback; 104pp; 203×127mm; 978-0-9926485-0-3; August 2013

The Fire in Me Now by Michael Curtis
Paperback; 90pp; 203×127mm; 978-0-9926485-4-1; August 2014

Short of Breath by Vivien Jones
Paperback; 102pp; 203×127mm; 978-0-9926485-5-8; October 2014

Cold Light of Morning by Julian Colton
Paperback; 90pp; 203×127mm; 978-0-9926485-7-2; March 2015

Automatic Writing by John Brewster
Paperback; 96pp; 203×127mm; 978-0-9926485-8-9; July 2015

Zygote Poems by Richard Thomas
Paperback; 66pp; 178×127mm; 978-0-9932119-5-9; July 2015

Les Animots: A Human Bestiary by Gordon Meade, images by Douglas Robertson
Hardback; 166pp; 203×127mm; 978-0-9926485-9-6; December 2015

Memorandum: Poems for the Fallen by Vanessa Gebbie
Paperback; 90pp; 203×127mm; 978-0-9932119-4-2; February 2016

The Light Box by Rosie Jackson
Paperback; 108pp; 203×127mm; 978-0-9932119-7-3; March 2016

There Are No Foreign Lands by Mark Holihan
Paperback; 96pp; 203×127mm; 978-0-9932119-8-0; June 2016

After Hours by David Cooke
Paperback; 92pp; 203×127mm; 978-0-9957381-0-2; April 2017

Short stories

Canterbury Tales on a Cockcrow Morning by Maggie Harris
Paperback; 138pp; 203×127mm; 978-0-9568921-6-4; September 2012

As Long as it Takes by Maria C. McCarthy
Paperback; 168pp; 203×127mm; 978-0-9926485-1-0; February 2014

In Margate by Lunchtime by Maggie Harris
Paperback; 204pp; 203×127mm; 978-0-9926485-3-4; February 2015

The Lost of Syros by Emma Timpany
Paperback; 128pp; 203×127mm; 978-0-9932119-2-8; July 2015

Only the Visible Can Vanish by Anna Maconochie
Paperback; 158pp; 203×127mm; 978-0-9932119-9-7; September 2016

Who Killed Emil Kreisler? by Nigel Jarrett
Paperback; 208pp; 203×127mm; 978-0-9568921-1-9; November 2016

A Short History of Synchronised Breathing and other stories by Vanessa Gebbie
Paperback; 132pp; 203×127mm; 978-0-9568921-2-6; February 2017

Curious things

Digging Up Paradise: Potatoes, People and Poetry in the Garden of England by Sarah Salway
Paperback; 164pp; 203×203mm; 978-0-9926485-6-5; June 2014

Punk Rock People Management: A No-Nonsense Guide to Hiring, Inspiring and Firing Staff by Peter Cook
Paperback; 40pp; 210×148mm; 978-0-9932119-0-4; February 2015

Do it Yourself: A History of Music in Medway by Stephen H. Morris
Paperback; 504pp; 229×152mm; 978-0-9926485-2-7; April 2015

The Music of Business: Business Excellence Fused with Music by Peter Cook
Paperback; 318pp; 210×148mm; 978-0-9932119-1-1; May 2015

The Hungry Writer by Lynne Rees
Paperback; 246pp; 244×170mm; 978-0-9932119-3-5; September 2015

The Ecology of Everyday Things by Mark Everard
Hardback; 126pp; 216×140mm; 978-0-9932119-6-6; November 2015

Lightning Source UK Ltd.
Milton Keynes UK
UKOW05f0602240617
303985UK00002B/37/P